D1825619

Glass House Books

We Who Decide

Henry Johnston, Australian author, essayist, and poet, was born in the UK in 1951. He is a contributor to both The Australian Independent Media Network and Independent Australia. In his career, Johnston served as an ABC Radio producer, speechwriter, and senior policy adviser. In the Independent Australia 2023 writing competition, his essay "In The Company of Giants", won the Most Compelling Article award. Other pieces of work encompass the short story "An Upturned Sky" (Stringybark Publishing), and an anthology *Port Out Starboard Home*, which was released as an eBook on Smashwords. He has written two novellas: *Best and Fairest* and *The Last Voyage of Aratus and Other Stories*. Set in inner-city Sydney during the 1960s, *Best and Fairest* chronicles the lives of 13 young men united by their love of Rugby League. In *The Last Voyage of Aratus and Other Stories*, Samuel Taylor Coleridge's *The Rime of the Ancient Mariner* is given a modern twist. His current project is a collection of poetry called The Gardens of Stone.

Glass House Books
Brisbane

We Who Decide

The interpretation of nightmares

Henry Johnston

Glass House Books
an imprint of IP (Interactive Publications Pty Ltd)
Treetop Studio • 9 Kuhler Court
Carindale, Queensland, Australia 4152
sales@ipoz.biz
http://ipoz.biz/shop
First published by IP in 2024
© 2024 Henry Johnston (text); IP (design)

Printed in 14 pt Avenir Book on Caslon Pro 12 pt.

ISBN: 9781922830876 (PB) 9781922830883 (eBook)

A catalogue record for this book is available from the National Library of Australia

NATIONAL LIBRARY OF AUSTRALIA

Author's Note

We Who Decide is a work of fiction. While names, characters and incidents are the product of my imagination, some events, people and businesses are based on fact and portrayed, as far as possible, in a positive light. Any resemblance to other persons, living or dead, is purely coincidental. Certain existing institutions, agencies and public offices are mentioned, but the characters described are fictitious. Foreign words, phrases, alternate spelling conventions and historical events unfold throughout the narrative; however, readers should not regard these, or linguistic and religious depictions, as wholly accurate.

– Henry Johnston

Acknowledgements

Front cover artwork: Dobrila Stamenkovic, Self-portrait of artist and photographer
Author photo: Henry Johnston
Book design: David P. Reiter

Tom Flood, manuscript assessor; Adam Finlay, editor at Writefish Professional Writing & Editing; author Don Defenderfer; poet James Gering and author Anne Howell.

My research for *We Who Decide* started in Vienna in 2014, coinciding with the 100th anniversary of the start of World War One. I immersed myself in Vienna's culture by visiting museums, galleries, libraries, cinemas, monuments, and significant landmarks. Amongst other things I traced the walking route mentioned in Chapter 4, followed the carriage route described in the penultimate chapter, and explored the village of Rust in the final chapter. Furthermore, I conducted secondary research in Romania, Bulgaria, the Czech Republic, and Hungary. I explored the vast CriticalPast collection, one of the world's largest royalty free visual archives, and immersed myself in countless newsreels and publications from the era. Much of the detail described in Chapter 8 comes courtesy of several courses conducted by WEA Sydney.

To the memory of two comrades-in-art:
John Conomos and Rosemary Laing

Contents

1 Arrival

Last night I dreamt my old maths tutor, Frau Sonke, scraped her crimson fingernails across the blackboard as a prelude to a smack with a cane across my knuckles. I woke from a tipsy sleep and hurled the feather pillow onto the cabin floor. Then, touching knees to chin, I slipped into a fitful doze on a fearful sea.

The crisp air of the Great Australian Bight had changed during the evening's champagne, dancing and inconclusive chess tournament. But now, enveloped in a humid fug, I play an unsettling game of 'What if?'

An orange glow fills the cabin's porthole, framing a perfect circle around the sun rising from the Tasman Sea. A toneless scrape reminds me of the opening bars of Strauss's *Einleitung, oder Sonnenaufgang*[1] performed by the Vienna Court Opera. I whisper, 'Speak English', though still it ties my tongue. Stylised handshakes and exaggerated eye rolls, à la Josephine Baker, grant me a moment to find the correct word. Men seem to adore these cutesy-tootsie flutters, but women see through my strategy. As for my assistant Leo Hubler, the contradictions of English syntax are difficult, and I scold him whenever he speaks German.

I wash my feet and legs beneath a tepid trickle of brackish water in the cramped shower recess and splash the last of my *Kölnisch Wasse*[2] across my torso and neck.

The breakfast xylophone chimes a greeting to the hungry. Coffee and dry crackers, a slice of fruit, a boiled egg perhaps, but thoughts of food set the stomach butterflies aflutter. No matter.

---

[1] *Also Sprach Zarathustra*
[2] cologne

The liner is due to dock by six this evening and by then someone or something will dislodge my fear of the unknown.

A stroll might settle nerves, but my fellow travellers have snared vantage points on the railings and stare westward at the haze-shrouded horizon. In the Port of Fremantle, my mental images of Australia proved unrealistic, but, with journey's end imminent, the terrors that prompted my flight from Europe roil as pixilated pictures. The dazzling Australian sky seems to drain the colour from my memories.

Leo knocks a rapid coded triplet.

'It's open.'

'*Weißt du, was zum Teufel dieses Summen ist?*'[3]

'English, Leo! How many times must I tell you, and no, I don't know what this buzz is, but it's driving me insane!'

'I thought deaf I am going,' Leo says.

'I am going deaf,' I reply, emphasising each word.

'Pardon?'

'Never mind, I'll ask someone. There's bound to be an answer.'

Leo's presence is reassuring, but my recollection of our final tense meeting in Papa's office to plan our escape is indistinct. And though today marks the climax of events which brought us to this point of latitude and longitude, I realise I cannot recall the features of my father's face.

A needle-sharp sun prickles the back of my neck. I return to the cabin for my pillbox hat, scarf and sunglasses before walking to the dining compartment. Waiters preen. I tap twice on the white linen tablecloth for a double measure of black coffee. Leo piles cheese and smoked meat atop two hot bread rolls. I crumble a dried cracker and mix the debris into yellow yolk. A pinch of pepper, a touch of Tabasco and a tap for more hot black coffee signals the magnitude of my hangover.

A purser pushes back two heavy swing doors.

'Good morning, Miss Lieder.'

---

[3] Do you know what the hell this buzz is?

'Excuse me, Herr Purser. May we speak?'

Leo excuses himself and returns to the buffet table for more delicacies.

'Call me John.'

'Thank you, John – and you may call me Susan. Can you tell me please the cause of the hum which fills the air above our ship?'

John sits opposite and calls for tea.

'You'll get used to it and after a while you won't notice them,' he says, counting three spoons of sugar into the hot, black liquid.

'Them? Who are they, please?'

'Cicadas.'

I decline his offer of an unfiltered cigarette and rummage for the word s'cardas, but all I can manage is a vague recollection of a similar tone I heard during a summer holiday in the Greek village Faros, on Ikaria.

'Insects, Miss Lieder.' John ashes into a clean tray and blows at the steam coiling from the sweetened beverage. 'Like grasshoppers, but different. You must have them in Europe. The noise tapers off as the sun gets higher, but these buggers are Green Grocers, the loudest insect on earth. There are hundreds of species. Let me think.' He counts on his fingers. 'There's the Brown Baker and the Cherry Nose, the Yellow Monday and the Red Eye, the Whisky Drinker and the Double Drummer and the Black Prince, and lots more.'

'But to hear the sound this far out to sea!'

'We are closer to the shore than it appears. The heat haze makes the land seem a long way off, but we are making good time and scheduled to sail through the Heads about noon or one o'clock.

'I'd better go. Might see you at lunch,' John says and, after a slurp of tea and leaving behind the ground-out remnants of a cigarette stub, he disappears back behind the swinging doors.

'So?' Leo asks between bites of poached egg and cornichon.

3

'*Zikaden. Millionen von ihnen.*'[4]

'*Oh, Ich verstehe.*'[5] Leo throws the stub of the uneaten pickle onto his plate.

'I have no appetite after this news,' he says, leaning the chair backward onto its rear two legs.

'All will be well, Leo. Trust me. We have discussed this a hundred times. Ashton Frost is meeting us, and we stay with him until my contract begins. He is bound to have a post for you. When I am settled, we will work together and continue as though nothing happened.'

But despite a welter of correspondence, and during my London meeting, I didn't mention a personal assistant. And while Ashton Frost lobbied contacts in Australia House to smooth the way for my engagement, other than outbound travel documents, I did not arrange similar for Leo. Instead, I passed three excruciating hours with the forger Wolfson in an upstairs garret of a shop in Stamford Hill. Papa warned me of his Roman hands and Russian fingers but forgot to mention his overpowering halitosis. Nevertheless, I paid him a fortune for my new birth certificate, citing my surname as Lieder. Wolfson settled on Gibraltar as my British Overseas Territories locale of birth and used church records for the date and the name of the priest who sanctified my baptism. Leo's Czech identity papers were also flawless, or so it seemed.

'Be calm, dear Leo.'

A pilot comes aboard, as a fleet of working vessels pass close by. Vertical smoke plumes attest a hot, windless morning.

Stern-faced porters clatter about the decks preparing for docking. All vestiges of familiarity nurtured during the six-week voyage vanish. Apart from families, those not affiliated with the ship experience emotions from excitement to loneliness.

The buzzing disguises the sound of waves crashing against

---

[4] Cicadas. Millions of them.
[5] Oh, I see.

the base of cliffs, so close that I feel I can touch the sandstone crags. But when I expect we are about to turn left past an immense cleft, we continue northward toward the further shore. The swell sloshes the exposed port side before we finally turn westward into the Heads. Spray drenches those gathered on lower decks. Some laugh, others experience the rising of the dead slow vessel in the pit of their stomach. The oppressive saloons offer no respite, but within minutes the pitching gives way and rolling waves trail off to a calm turquoise.

The hum pulses against the wooded northern and southern shores. Flocks of large, yellow-crested white birds screech and circle above. As we inch deeper into the harbour, woodland gives way to clusters of clapboard houses clinging limpet-like to gilded rocks. Purples and fiery reds weave into manicured lawns and coil toward shoreline beaches. A cerulean haze shimmies the air.

One day I will paint this scene in the style of Seurat's *The Channel of Gravelines*, which I studied in St Tropez.

Small yachts jostle before scudding into distant bays and reaches, as part of a regatta. Lighters, ferries, tugs and barges cross and crisscross each other's wakes amidst a chorus of toots and bellows.

The whine coruscates. A sonic murmuration. Chirruping green and red dart-like birds call and respond in flight. Dark shapes swim alongside the bow, as the westing sun bathes the looming city's sandstone buildings with a coppery sheen.

Leo points toward a knot of beefy men, dressed in heavy serge uniforms, others in khaki. The unsmiling officials walk the decks before moving into the darkened cargo holds.

John speaks into a megaphone.

'Passengers are reminded to pack belongings and ensure travel papers are ready for inspection. Because of wartime regulations, Customs and Immigration checks are being processed aboard ship while we wait for a berth in Darling Harbour. Disembarkation begins once these formalities finish.'

Gripe grips my stomach.

The breakfast saloon is converted into a utilitarian interview chamber. Calico screens hide the trappings of opulence. French jardinières, gilded mirrors and plush velvet chaise lounges disappear. Tables, stripped of starched white cloths, reveal stains and age marks. Similar spaces also transformed unmask the glamour of luxury cruising as a sleight of hand.

When I embarked at Tilbury, I boarded a dream liner designed to sail the oceans of a vivacious world. I believed the Phoney War would never end. What could happen aboard a ship where the day begins with a fresh gardenia placed in my cabin? I had passed fun-filled weeks in the company of people whose speech, clothing, manners and behaviour reflected the status of my family. Now this link with my past life is disappearing.

Ships' officers and senior staff speak an incomprehensible dialect and Petty Officer John typifies this conundrum. Fellow voyagers, as fluent in English as me, comprehend about one in five words. As the ship's management complies with the demands of Australian military and immigration officials, we passengers remain clueless about what to do next.

Bureaucrats swarm through cabins, poking bags, prodding bound parcels, speaking with voices raised as if addressing uncomprehending children, over-emphasising the need to follow this or that request. Their London counterparts had been polite, touching their hat brims when speaking with passengers. No such niceties among the Australian officials who are unblinking, firm, suspicious and aggressive.

A group of officials circles Leo. One fellow traces the details of his travel documents with a slow-moving forefinger, while another unbuckles his portmanteau.

I sense Leo doesn't know what is happening and edge to his side.

'Not so fast, missy,' the official says. 'Do you know this man? Well, do you? Come on, speak up. I haven't got all day.'

The contents of Leo's sea chest spill onto a table. Three officers unfold his clothes and feel the seams of ironed shirts and trousers. I panic. What if they find the gold sewn into the lining encircling the interior? But the searchers concentrate on contents and ignore the structure of the stout chest.

'Yes, we are travelling companions,' I reply.

'But he is not your husband or a relative, is he?'

'No.'

'Then why are you speaking on his behalf?' the officer demands, tapping his hobnailed boot. 'Well?'

Leo struggles with the rapid-fire questions.

A senior official carrying a full-sized edition of *The Times Atlas of the World* motions him to sit. The junior agent, who, with outstretched forefinger had examined Leo's travel papers, repeats the same gesture in another book. I cannot read its cover title, but I recognise two words: Cheb and Eger. The latter word is the German name of the city, county and government district of a town renamed to the Czech, Cheb, but not listed in the atlas.

Wolfson had assured me UK authorities deemed Czechs friendly and chose Cheb as Leo's home, but he, as with most Europeans, underestimated the significance of the region's German-speaking population.

'His documents are valid, sir, but, according to this list, Cheb is in the Sudetenland, which is now part of the German Reich, so he's German, not Czechoslovakian, and an enemy alien.'

I shout at Leo.

'Keep it down, missy. Your turn will come in a sec.'

Similar combative acts erupt at tables in various sections of the saloon. Frustrated people plead to be released. Women faint. Children sulk and scream with frustration. The drone grows louder as we pass underneath a great, grey bridge.

'Please, John, can you find my friend?'

'Anything for you, Miss Lieder,' John says with a wink, and clicks his tongue, as if encouraging a recalcitrant horse.

'We will decide who comes to Australia, and I'm the one who makes the decision as to where you and your Hun friend go, missy.'

I suppress an urge to slap the pimply-faced inspector. Instead, I ask, 'What is your name?'

'Nicholas Treloar, missy. Now do as you are told, or you'll never get off this rust bucket.'

John returns to my side, but a waved finger warns him to be silent.

'Your friend is an enemy alien, missy, and that means he's gunna take a long train ride.'

The blank-faced purser stares at me, but when the official in the ill-fitting uniform moves toward another erupting fracas, John slips a cardboard chit into my hand.

'This is your friend's registration number. The immigration boss told me he'll be transported to a new internment camp being built in the town of Hay. Don't lose it,' he says.

Setting sunlight scorches the saloon a hot, acrid red.

I stand among a dwindling few, desperate to be free of the confines of the sweltering ship.

The trio of officials who dealt with Leo now read Ashton's correspondence guaranteeing my employment in the Frost Emporium as a fashion couturiere. At last, official stamps festoon the pages of my passport and sundry documents.

'May I go to meet Mr Ashton Frost?'

'Not tonight, missy. You're off to Larpa. Mr Frost can contact you there after we interview him about your stay. Oh, and a late happy twenty-first birthday to you.'

Weighed down by baggage, I clamber along the rickety gangplank and follow directions toward an ancient Dennis omnibus. As the vehicle splutters for the exit, I read a word on a street sign – Ultimo – and pluck its meaning from my growing vocabulary. Ultimo means in or of the month preceding the present.

Through the din of graunching clutch and stinking exhaust, I speak in German. '*An diesem dem 12. Ultimo, habe ich Champagner getrunken und den 18. Geburtstag meines anderen Lebens gefeiert.*'[6]

---

[6] On this, the twelfth ultimo, I drank champagne and celebrated the eighteenth birthday of my other life.

2 Red, White, Red

My father, Maximillian Liebler, began his morning constitutional on the Penzinger Straße,[7] then walked past Embassy Row, before taking a brisk stroll through Auer-Welsbach Park. On mornings when I accompanied him, Papa paused after crossing the boulevard and, with hand on heart, turned toward the Schönbrunn Palace with a formal bow, to bid a silent 'good morning' to the memory of the old emperor.

Papa began this tribute to Franz Joseph after surviving the terrible Ninth Battle of the Isonzo against the Italians in November 1916, in the weeks before the grand aristocrat's death. Fidelity to the emperor prompted my parents to buy the estate on Penzinger. Within its leafy confines we celebrated a life of good fortune as proud subjects of a monarch who gave succour to all his peoples, both near and as far as the borders of the Pale of Settlement.

Papa always wore a sprig of alpine Edelweiss, the insignia of his regiment of the Imperial Hunters, and an important element of his ritual. I wove the small white flower heads into a dense cluster so precise only touch could reveal it as an imitation. I am Shoshanna, Susan in English, Maximillian Liebler's only daughter. Either my mother Ruth or I pinned the totem to his lapel, impossible for him to do so now since the loss of the first joints of his fore and second fingers from frostbite during military service in the Tyrolean trenches.

Teeming summer rain thwarted Papa's morning walk in those fatalistic hours, so a comfortable chair by the wireless listening to the BBC World Service served as a suitable substitute.

Papa heeded my brother Rudolph's advice to be sceptical

---

[7] Penzinger Street

of the domestic press. Editorial bias, Rudolph said, had grown conspiratorial since the calamity of the brief, bloody civil war. Rudolph said the Austrian press barons had abandoned impartial reporting in the tense days after Chancellor Dollfuss suspended parliament in 1933.

Any type of trade with Italian clients, and Dollfuss's obvious fascination with fascism, spiked my father's blood pressure. The trusted BBC News service detailed the breadth of Dollfuss's political naivety, which led to the slaughter of hard-line socialists holed up in the nation's Red redoubts. The majority of casualties fell in Vienna's Karl Marx Tenement in the 19th district. According to my father, far better to establish a détente with the former President of Parliament Karl Renner, and the socialists – who numbered about half the population – than shoot them.

My father, brother and mother, along with thousands of like-minded citizens, abhorred Dollfuss's authoritarian world view.

Papa championed liberalism over mindless discipline. The wanton destruction of the centrepiece of Red Vienna shook his faith in the possibility of a secure Austria. This tenement building, inpired by Otto Wagner, an architect Papa lauded above all members of the Vienna Secession, crumbled under a barrage of shellfire.

And though much had changed since the fall of the Habsburgs, my father admired the early initiatives of Karl Renner. As a veteran, he welcomed the introduction of state aid for disabled ex-soldiers, who had lost limbs or the use of lungs from phosgene gas. But, from the time of Dollfuss's ascendancy, Papa recounted a growing pessimism amongst old comrades in arms and close associates.

I watched the golden days of the last century fade with the steel grey tones flecking his goatee and thinning hair. But life continued. An unselfish son, the love of his life and, dare I say, me, imbued Papa with a determination to keep the Liebler enterprise safe from travails. And London beckoned.

My father gave me the nickname ZaSu, in honour of his favourite American actor ZaSu Pitts.

I planted a "good morning" kiss on his whiskered cheek.

'Where are you off to in this downpour, my dear?'

'Today, I begin lessons for Schubert's *Fantasia in F Minor* – your favourite,' I said, massaging the stumps of his fingers. 'And I intend to keep you to your promise to play with me.' He laughed and tickled my ribs. I giggled and tickled him back. We knew Schubert wrote his piano fantasia for four hands.

'Have Leo walk with you, and be back in time for lunch,' he said.

I crossed my eyes, fish-pursed my lips for a second peck on his cheek, donned an outsized Macintosh and rubber boots, then, standing below an enormous umbrella held aloft by Leo, disappeared into the rain.

Despite his simple joy, I knew of my father's heartache. One afternoon, I overheard him say to my mother, 'I wonder what Henriette would have made of her little sister had she lived?'

Papa often recalled my eldest sister Henriette, named after the doyen of early Berlin literary salons Henriette Herz. I recall him telling my mother all he could remember of Henriette was holding her tiny coffin.

An acquaintance of Papa from a popular café remarked over an apéritif that the Spanish Flu arrived in Europe, courtesy of one of Woodrow Wilson's doughboys.

Whatever its origin, my sister's death filched a piece of Papa's soul and robbed my parents of lifelong happiness.

'Turn on the radio,' Rudolph said, as he helped Papa tune the dial into a stronger signal.

> This is the BBC. Reports from our correspondent
> in Vienna allege the Austrian Chancellor Engelbert
> Dollfuss has been shot in the city's chancellery

building, the venue of the famous Vienna Congress.

Ruth rushed into the parlour, placed an arm around my father's shoulder, and pulled Rudolph to her side.

'Troops are cordoning off the inner ring,' Leo said, as I jostled into the centre of my huddled family.

'Did you lock the gates?' Rudolph asked.

'Yes sir,' Leo said.

'Check the petrol in the town car and fill it up if it is low. Unlock the Mausers. Pack ammunition clips into two haversacks: one for you and one for me. I want the lot ready to go if we need to leave quickly. Understand?'

'What about the household staff?'

Rudolf beckoned Ruth, who caught Leo's eye and nodded assent. Rudolf mouthed the words, 'Drive them.'

The morning melted to a hot, clammy noon and a glorious summer day – perfect for a visit to the Konditorei Kaiser ice cream parlour for orange sorbet with chocolate sprinkles, but not today.

Rudolf turned away a stream of father's friends and associates, seeking solace or an explanation. 'It is too dangerous to be outdoors,' he said.

Rudolph also persuaded my parents to acknowledge an impending calamity after the attempt on the Chancellor's life, but my mother wanted none of it, and Papa, a stickler for protocol said, 'This is a time for reflection.'

I broke the impasse. 'His nickname is Dullfeet,' I said.

'How dare you,' mother exclaimed.

'Who calls him Dullfeet?' Maximillian demanded.

'Dullfeet or the Jockey, he is a figure of fun,' Rudolf said in my defence.

'That's enough,' Maximillian said, but Rudolf persisted.

'Dollfuss takes his orders from Mussolini, who follows the Pope's instructions. The Vatican imposed corporatism on

Austria because their puppet, Dollfuss, is too stupid to devise an original political idea.'

'There will be no comments like this in my house,' Maximillian said. 'Dollfuss is a patriot. He deserves our respect for his military and public service, so no more if you please.'

Yet he did not deny the truth of my brother's observations. Papa feared a build-up of Italian troops on the Austrian border once word of the Chancellor's fate reached Mussolini in Rome.

Mindful of an even greater threat from within the state, and ugly developments festering in Germany, Rudolf implored my parents to at least heed his suggestions. 'We need a plan of escape,' he said.

As afternoon faded to evening, Papa listened in silence to Rudolph's summation.

My family's enterprise is The House of Liebler. We design and manufacture uniforms for the Austro-Hungarian military, its police, and sundry civil services, and have done so since before the Napoleonic Wars.

Rudolf, with the help of the family's personal assistant Leo Hulbert, purchases and ships stocks of furs and animal pelts from merchants based in the Ukrainian port city Odessa.

My mother and I supervise a team of designers, colourists, weavers, artisans and milliners. A cohort of workers follow our creations, and we manufacture and supply a multitude of differing styles of dress uniforms to the servants of a nation and a culture which traces its roots to the origins of the Holy Roman Empire. And I also devise ready-made affordable fashion lines for export across Europe and England, and soon, as far away as Australia.

As a prisoner of war, Papa recalled the worst of the Italian insults: *soldatini di cioccolato*[8] – a sneering reference to the bewildering variety of uniforms worn by Austrian troops.

During that long sultry afternoon, Rudolph detailed his plan

---

[8] chocolate box soldiers

to devolve the business into the supervision of a covey of trusted bureaucrats. Thus secured and ratified at law, my family could retire to the comfort and safety of our estate in Surrey, and, if worse came to worst, we might secure a foothold in Australia, a move with real potential if my employment with the Frost Family Enterprise proved successful.

A late evening BBC bulletin confirmed the worst: a gang of Nazi thugs had assassinated Dollfuss in an attempted putsch.

Weeks later, Mussolini's troops smashed an uprising in the alpine Austrian province of Carinthia. Mussolini warned the fledgling German chancellor he would wage war to possess regions of the former empire he coveted.

The remnants of the crumbling Austro-Hungarian empire continued to unravel as if tangled threads falling from a broken, spinning loom.

Franz Joseph's former subjects splintered into social and cultural factions, which the Goths, Vandals and Huns of antiquity would have recognised as their tribal offspring.

Before bedtime, Papa calmed Rudolph with a honeyed promise to consider his plan. And I learnt from a crony of my father who somehow managed to enter the estate that my exclusive client Vera von Babenhausen, for whom I had sketched hats for this year's summer season, had accepted a marriage proposal. Armed with this news and in the spirit of the old Habsburg saying, 'Let others wage war, but thou oh happy Austria, marry,' I was determined to create the finest haute couture for the soon-to-be bride of the eleventh Chancellor of Austria, the authoritarian Kurt Schuschnigg.

3 Odessa

Leo told me he loved Odessa above all the Black Sea ports of Europe and Asia Minor. After journeying from Bratislava, he and my brother Rudolph boarded a north-bound freighter in Constanta Romania, avoiding Turkish ports because of the ruinous rates of bribery. From Odessa, they planned a visit to Sevastopol to inspect a consignment of luxurious animal skins shipped down the Volga from the Soviet city renamed in Stalin's honour.

Rumour suggested steppe polecat and European mink, plentiful in Batumi, Georgia. Demand for red fox and souslik soared in the bustling markets of the dangerous Bulgarian town of Varna. Securing black bear hides meant a trip to Novorossiysk, but none of these cities compared with Odessa which, according to Rudolph, is as seductive as its founder, Catherine the Great.

Leo visited a brothel and a hashish parlour where he bought a half kilo of the pungent tarry drug, flecked throughout with white Afghani opium. Outside in the bright sun, a throng of people dressed in raiment worthy of Gustav Klimt promenaded on the Prokhorovsky Square. In a mellow dope haze, Leo joined Armenians, Tartars, Azeris, Tajiks, Balts, Turkmen, Persians, Russians, Frenchmen, dark-eyed Romanians, Jews, Italians, Chinese, Mongols, Afghans, and others partaking in the city's myriad delights.

Depending on the time of year, the Pryvoz Market offered a cornucopia grown in the rich soil of Russian and Asian river deltas. Driven by hashish hunger, Leo devoured Uzbek melons and flat circular Anatolian peaches, but the aroma of Fesenjan-Persian pomegranate and walnut stew truly set him salivating.

The Pryvoz alleys teemed with thieves and tricksters. As

throat singers warbled for a kopeck, sneering Turkmen shoved emaciated children toward passers-by, backhanding them if they failed to snag a client. Russians, mostly Cossacks, whirled across sabres, dancing the knee-snapping *prisyadka*[9] and slashing at grumbling Ukrainians who spat in their direction.

Soviet officials hiked up taxes and skimmed fortunes for their lavish *dachas*, built along beachfronts north and south of the city. Despite the impost, Odessa offered merchants difficult-to-get items. Unless they were prepared to travel overland to the steppe of Central Asia, it was impossible to buy its greatest prize, Karakul fleece.

Rudolph had heard a rumour of a large quantity of the tightly curled skin of newborn Karakul lambs, many cut from the wombs of pregnant ewes. Ushanka headwear is but one use of this prized animal skin, but a Soviet apparatchik had impounded the pelts, which had been hauled by a caravan of Bactrian camels from Astrakhan to Novorossiysk. It seemed the comrade was desperate to offload the treasure trove but had set an astronomical price in gold.

Rudolph passed word into the endless Odessa chatter mill, saying he would inspect the consignment and make a fair offer. A dozen ink wash drawings by me, displaying the panoply of colours of the skins, guaranteed sales in Paris, Milan and New York for five times or more than the agreed price.

Neither Rudolph, a moustachioed, agile man and expert fencer, nor Leo, with the build of a bare-knuckled boxer, had qualms about despatching thieves. Kill or be killed: the unspoken law of Black Sea ports.

Leo said every deal in Odessa was a potential trap, and conversations were routinely eavesdropped, so to let down one's guard meant death or worse: to be sold as a slave to an Ottoman pasha and entourage.

---

[9] a Russian dance

Generations of men, women and children living on the European shores of the Black and Mediterranean seas feared and detested Ottoman Turks. Thus had it been since 1529 when a victorious army of knights of the Holy Roman Empire stopped the Ottoman's march into Europe and dumped thousands of corpses into the Danube, after the failed Siege of Vienna. Now descendants of the Crimean Zaporozhian Cossack Horde ran the local criminal syndicates and proved every bit as cruel as the Ottoman Turks.

Following Odessa's declaration as an open port, this key city of the Ukrainian Soviet became the playground of gangsters, freebooters and traders.

Years of commercial experience enabled Rudolph to develop a knack for coded conversation across a wide range of acquaintances. He sought clues such as the volume of rain which fell across the Caucasus during this or that year, or the depth of snow covering Mount Elbrus. Had sandstorms swept in from the Gobi or did the air remain calm in a particular season? The nuance of an answer informed a mental calculus of the quantity of a species thriving in a certain region.

With this knowledge Rudolph did not need to specify the animal. Precise information about terrain, climate and atmospheric anomalies enabled him to make a realistic offer and predict the price a vendor might accept. The doyens of Pryvoz respected Rudolph, who rarely failed to winkle out the raw stock in constant demand by the leading Western fashion houses. But the Soviet bureaucrats proved worse than the old Czarist palatines and pretended to be immune to the enticement of a reasonable gratuity, especially after the famishment of the Holodomor, Stalin's deliberate terror famine of Ukraine. The spectre of starvation made for dotted i's and crossed t's, or their Cyrillic equivalents, amongst lower-ranked Soviet apparatchiks.

Tea room habitués told Rudolph the number one comrade boasting about a huge stock of Karakul fleece owed a fortune in gambling debts, but Leo remained suspicious. Instinct about the Soviets and other rogues made him indispensable to the House of Liebler, which he joined as a watchful youth working by his mother's side on the tannery sorting tables. The shop steward and the supervisor had noted Leo's proficiency for spotting flawed leather. As a curious teen, Leo fell in with a band of old French communards who had returned to their trades in the garment industry after fleeing to Vienna after the Franco-Prussian War.

A wunderkind in most languages except English, Leo followed the arguments published by the Frenchies in cheap pamphlets and distributed in the workshops and factories. As if untangling the fibres of knotted fleece, Leo charted the machinations of various Bolshevik cabals and understood the labyrinthine disputes of the First International of May 1905, but fair pay and good conditions tempered any inclination to join the Reds.

This understanding of the motivations behind workshop disputes impressed Rudolph, as did Leo's physical strength, fearlessness and general aptitude. I trusted Leo from the moment we met, and my respect for him proved good enough for my big brother.

Physical strength and cunning meant both men held a fair chance of surviving the murderous world of Russian gangsters and the operatives of the People's Commissariat for Internal Affairs, the NKVD. Odessa, like all cities of the USSR, endured the terrors of a secret police force whose members announced their presence by flashing a badge with the emblem of a dagger piercing the Hammer and Sickle.

Leo warned Rudolph the Soviet customs official touting the Karakul lambskins was an NKVD informer. 'He's bound to be on the take,' Leo said.

'And he'll have friends lurking in the shadows,' Rudolph replied, before asking for the address.

'Near the old Khadjibey Fortress. Surrounded by forest. Not my favourite part of Odessa.'

'I'll wear a vest, but I will bring only half. I'll have a similar amount in the money pouch.'

'Do you think that is enough?'

'As a temptation, yes,' Rudolph said. 'The balance is settled if he delivers the cargo with authorised stamped papers to the dock. Extra clips for the Mausers and sharpen your poniard.'

'Goes without saying, but what do we do with the rest?'

'The catacombs.'

Rudolph had uncovered an innocuous steel cover on Kartamyshevska Street in the Moldavanka District, which opened into Odessa's old stone mine tunnels and coiled for miles under the city.

My father had purchased a detailed Cyrillic map of the catacombs from an old ex-British Army officer who claimed it as a trophy from a dead Czarist engineer during the Crimean War. No matter its origin, Rudolph substantiated its value by pre-dawn visits to the site. The map showed a reinforced caisson concealed underfoot and covered in mud and shit. Underneath lay four ashlar slabs, metres from the entry point into the maze.

A length of chain and a crowbar lying on a pile of rubble, plus a lewis pin inserted into the lewis hole – *et voilà* – entry to a subterranean cell within the miles of catacombs. Impossible to find the chamber without a map unless the searcher knew precisely where to look and how to use the antique lifting tools.

Rudolph wrapped the British gold coins in sheets of oilcloth and hid them in a nondescript nook in the catacombs. And, although confident of the gold's security, the impending deal reeked of treachery.

Leo said that my brother insisted on a daylight inspection of the lambskins, but, as expected, the commissar did not approach the building until dusk. A gang of unannounced accomplices meant robbery. Rudolph watched the front of the building through a pair of small, high-powered binoculars. Leo staked out the rear. Five men approached, but three took cover in the underbrush.

Leo would shoot them if they moved toward the meeting, and Rudolph would kill the commissar and his deputy.

'You are late,' Rudolph said.

'Fuck you.'

'Charming. So, explain why I should deal with you after you insult me?'

'I am joking,' the commissar said, unlocking the doors. 'Look inside.'

Rudolph sniffed the air, seeking the familiar odour of lanolin, but this lot did not emit the tell-tale smell. Bokhara black bear and fox, but not Karakul lamb.

'There is nothing here that interests me.' Rudolph stood his ground.

'Come in and have a closer look, Jew. The Karakul is at the rear.'

'Trotsky's a Jew, Commissar.'

'Fuck you, and fuck Trotsky.'

'And Karl Marx was a Jew, so fuck you,' Rudolph said, as his slim fighting knife pierced the commissar's heart.

The bodyguard blew a whistle. Rudolph failed to notice the swinging club which broke his clavicle, but nervous strength enabled a single slash on the throat, severing the bodyguard's jugular.

Three cracks from Leo's Mauser were the last sound Rudolph heard before unconsciousness.

Leo popped an ammonium carbonate capsule and slapped Rudolph's face until he came to and screamed in pain.

'Get your vest off,' Leo said, but Rudolph passed out again. Leo let him be. He felt a sensation of floating above his body, watching a sequence of movements calculated to save their lives.

Leo freed Rudolph's still warm money vest – impossible had he been conscious and screaming in pain – strapped it to his own chest, took the other money pouch, inspected the broken bone, and fashioned a hunter's sling, cobbled from whatever he could find. Once complete, he popped another ammonium carbonate cap and shook sense into my groaning brother. Then he dragged the commissar's body to the site of the three dead goons, propped the still bleeding, heavy-set corpse of the bodyguard onto a pallet, and with a fireman's lift, ran toward the other bodies.

Twilight. Red eyes flashed in the trees.

Juvenile pack members whimpered, snarled and yelped, crazed from the scent of fresh blood, but the alpha wolf held them in check.

Leo rummaged through the dead men's pockets. Rubbish mostly, except for the commissar's Customs badge. So, who was this NKVD operative? But he found nothing to reveal the bastard's identity.

The stiletto glinted in the fading light. Bloody eyes popped out of sockets. Leo placed the bleeding organs onto the cheeks of each corpse to entice the steppe wolves to shred the faces first, making identification difficult. A grisly gift of extra time for a getaway.

Rudolph, fully conscious, staggered upright and rummaged for a bottle of vodka. 'Burn the bodies.'

'Too late,' Leo said, pointing at the wolf pack tearing the corpses and fighting over the bounty of bloody meat. 'Time to go.'

Leo poured the last of the vodka onto a piece of cloth and tossed the burning rag inside the warehouse. The smell of scorching skin scared, but did not drive off, the salivating wolves, determined to continue their grisly meal. But an NKVD insignia, tattooed onto the nape of the bodyguard's bloodied neck, survived their mauling.

Rudolph and Leo made it to their car. An orange glow flickered in the rear-view mirror.

A florin, passed to the hotel night porter, secured the house doctor who said, 'Let me guess, Pryvoz Markets.'

'Jumped by Turks,' Leo said.

By midnight, snores from the bandaged Rudolph filled the bedroom, thanks to an intravenous morphine injection.

The doctor cleared Rudolph for travel but declared heavy lifting out of the question for at least two months.

The gold coins remained in the underground nook.

Leo pestered the night porter for shipping departures to Constanta on the Romanian Black Sea coast. Nothing for a week, but a glut of expensive berths to Istanbul, with guaranteed onward transit to ports on the Adriatic and Mediterranean – for the right price, of course.

Leo booked two tickets for a noon departure to Trieste and waited for an amphetamine to work its magic on Rudolph.

'Istanbul? Fuck.'

'No choice,' Leo said to the pained, speeding Rudolph.

'Have you paid?'

'I'll settle up dockside.'

'Fetch the money belt.'

The bag of coinage told a special story.

'Notice anything different?'

'No,' Leo said, weighing and passing the bag to Rudolph.

'Good. No-one but an expert can tell.'

'It is gold?' Leo asked.

'Yes, but these,' Rudolph replied, tossing the bag into his good hand, 'are worth a fraction of their face value.'

Rudolph counted out coins onto a bureau and placed the rest into the leather pouch.

'Our London contact is a specialist. Each is the precise weight of a sovereign,' he said, 'but debased. An old Roman trick. A plug of cheap metal covered with gold leaf, then soaked in a bath of special chemicals, and impressed with a forged stamp. These are useless in the UK, but perfect for this part of the world. Everybody wants British currency. This lot,' he continued, 'will pay for our tickets, but you'll have to wear the vest. We'll get the real sovereigns on the next trip.'

'If there is a next trip,' said Leo.

'Oh, there will be,' Rudolph replied. 'Fuck the Turks, and the Bolsheviks while we're at it.'

'I'd rather not, thank you,' said Leo.

The porter collected their baggage and called a taxi to the Odessa Holovna Rail Station, but once inside the cab, Leo changed the destination to the Port of Odessa.

'Trust no-one,' he said.

'Who did that stupid Bolshevik think he was dealing with?' Rudolph said. 'When we get aboard, load up the hash pipe. My fucking shoulder is killing me.'

4 Degenerate art

The cortège for Papa's sister's funeral assembled at the passenger wharf below the Tabor Straße Bridge near Schwedenplatz. After the guests boarded, the barge chugged past factories on Vienna's outskirts. Foetid air melted into the sweet scent of newly mown hay. The steppe rolled east to Hungary, Romania and far-off Ukraine.

I watched a white bird peck at unseen things atop the ramparts of Devin Castle, where the Morava River meets the Danube, and wondered why a gull flew so far from the Black Sea.

We disembarked near Bratislava's old bridge, Starý Most, and climbed the palisade to the Jewish quarter. Grim-faced mourners tied the *kriah* ribbon to their clothes. The funeral was the last gathering of my extended family, but at the time I yearned to escape the gloom of the death of an aunt I barely knew and slipped away from the mute throng clustered on Zidovska.

The air was sharp as hoarfrost. My feet ached from the cold, but I was free from suffocating perfume and dusty face powder.

Stout doors buttressed dwellings along the length of Zidovska, camouflaging what lay behind each entrance. The gallery was somewhere hereabouts.

An intoxicating taboo parched my mouth. Strands of saliva streaked my lips. I made out the name in Cyrillic – Александр Родченко[10] – and put my shoulder to the heavy door and barged in as if a thief entering a temple.

I was alone. Hot air blew from a furnace. Lilya Brik's portrait stared from a wall. A spasm choked my lungs, and I felt I might

---

[10] Alexander Rodchenko

faint. I stood amidst examples of Rodchenko's Constructivism, classified by the Nazis as degenerate art.

Was I a degenerate?

I scanned the cheap paper poster and read an extract from the essay "From the Easel to the Machine" by Nikolai Tarabukin:

> But here the most bitter disillusionment and the most
> hopeless impasse awaited the artist and that fatal word
> for modern art, 'crisis', has never perhaps sounded so
> tragically as it does now.

A ticking clock chimed time to leave. I felt sweat on my palms. The art seemed to swirl off the walls. A petite Slovak girl nodded toward the visitors' book.

I signed as ZaSu and stumbled into the freezing air.

Mourners trudged behind the horse-drawn coffin and stopped seven times on the last journey to the cemetery.

A Carpathian wind rippled the surface of the Danube. Mama's ears and face hidden by a mink *ushanka* hat. Remorse reddened my cheeks, but no-one noticed, for, like Mama, my face was encircled by a scarf and a fur shield.

I whispered memorised snatches of the Tarabukin treatise and thought of the day when I would write my own manifesto:

> Works of this type include the spatially constructive
> works by The Society of Young Artists, the volumetric,
> non-planar constructions of Rodchenko, and the spatial
> paintings of Petr Miturich.

I barely understood the syntax, but I too was a young artist and determined to grow into its meaning.

In the evening, the mourners gathered in the lobby of a hotel facing Horsky Park. Blackbirds filled the air, chattering as they roosted in algid trees. Wan and strained relatives attempted to console my Papa, who had recited *Kaddish*[11] after the burial.

I made an excuse and retreated to my freezing apartment,

---

[11] prayers at the end of life

stripped and slid between starched white sheets, shivered, and pulled blankets over my head, but I couldn't get warm. Images of art spun in my mind's eye. Lilya Brik stared into my soul.

I caressed myself. The soles of my feet warmed. I clenched my buttocks and bit my lower lip.

Blackbirds cawed beyond the frost-covered window.

Who will say *Kaddish* for me?

5 Anschluss

My brother is clear-eyed, like Mama. He is also ruthless, although he keeps this aspect of his temperament in check and hidden from my parents. Rudolph is relaxed and comfortable in Leo's presence but reserved with his fencing partner friends. He learnt reticence from Papa, along with a sense of loyalty and conformity with social norms. These traits are mirror images of the best and worst of my father's personality. Both men can be insufferable and gregarious. Along with Leo, Rudolph and my father form the trinity of men in my life.

I could not recall an occasion when my Papa was indecisive, but he did not, or would not, heed Rudolph's urgings to depart immediately for London, preferably from Trieste on the Adriatic Sea.

Papa's aversion to all things Italian sprang from his wartime experiences, abetted by a contemporary loathing of *Il Duce*.[12] Rudolph argued the city of Trieste, with its German-speaking minority, the safest if only port from where our parents could embark. Zadar on the Dalmatian coast might work, but departing the Continent from a decrepit Illyrian city meant extra stopovers and fiddly transfers.

Papa agreed, but on the proviso he and Mama drive via Linz to visit his dead sister's family and help settle her affairs.

Rudolph had no comeback to this demand and agreed to the longer journey. He would time his return from a second trip to Odessa to reunite with our parents.

I planned to catch a train to Paris via Stuttgart, with a Channel crossing from Calais to Dover, leaving me plenty of time to meet with Ashton Frost, but at the last-minute Rudolph

---

[12] The leader: Benito Mussolini

convinced my parents Leo should be my escort.

'This is a sensible arrangement,' Mama said. 'Your father has an acquaintance in London who will help with travel documents. I am excited for you, my dearest Shoshanna. Your new contract will take our name around the world.'

Judging by his body language Leo had other ideas, but, before he could plead his case to return to Odessa, Rudolph cut him short.

'We have a fortune wrapped up in ZaSu's artwork. She is seventeen and needs an escort at least as far as the French border.'

'I can look after myself, brother,' I replied.

But Rudolph, with an insufferable sense of duty, said, 'I do not doubt it, sister. I am not worried about you, but the drawings and samples, plus the studio etchings, are far too valuable. Leo goes with you to England and Australia, and that is final.'

Leo glared at Rudolph. 'Do I get a say in this?'

'Of course you do, but hear me out. ZaSu is about to travel to another hemisphere. This is unprecedented for this family, including you, my friend. Apart from me, you are the only man in the world I trust to keep her safe. I've lost one sister, and I don't intend to lose another.'

After an awkward silence, both men nodded an invisible message between each other, which Leo later decoded for me after we boarded the Tilbury-bound steamer. Leo said my brother told him to use the Mauser on any Nazi thugs who got in our way. I am certain he would not have hesitated. I still recall the sound of that pistol dropping with a splash into the gasoline-streaked water of Calais before we sailed for England.

'I have one appointment in Odessa,' Rudolph said to Mama and Papa. 'In and out. We will keep in touch by telegram from our hotels and meet in Trieste.'

'Your mother and I will stay in the Savoia Excelsior Palace,' Papa said. 'The hotel architect Ladislaus Fiedler is an old friend.'

Mama, tears rolling down her cheeks, hugged and kissed me and Leo, and said, 'So, it is settled.'

These are the last words I remember my mother speaking.

Next morning, Leo and I boarded an overnight sleeper from the south railway station. My portfolio and a mountain of sundries, crated into wooden pallets, filled a sizable portion of a freight wagon. Each chest required a customs declaration with my name, seat and carriage number, destination, plus a list of all contents, with copies affixed in a prominent position for ease of scrutiny. I stored the paperwork in a valise, along with our tickets and passports. The Nazi Swastika over-stamped each manifest, smudging the official seal of the Austrian double-headed eagle. I stared at the twisted graffito.

This ugly blot also defiled telegrams from Ashton Frost, who proved a prolific sender of cables, compiled in curt, coded triplets. Ashton had despatched precise orders to me requesting designs for a multitude of goods made by our company, as well as monetary transmissions in British pounds, plus confirmation of my tenure with the Frost Emporium in Sydney.

I have treasured these flimsy chronicles, the box Brownie photographs and the postcards, throughout my life. They remain a day by day testament crammed into a shoe carton, which count down the months, weeks, days and minutes of the timeline to the Anschluss[13] of 12 March 1938.

Leo predicted a stop-start journey to Salzburg and beyond, but rail officials waived our westbound train through to accommodate countless eastbound German troop convoys deploying to Vienna, and all major Austrian cities, including Linz. Multiple divisions of soldiers crammed aboard these trains, into columns of trucks, and on horse-drawn wagons, and streamed across Austria's borders, to enforce the reality of a new Greater Germany. Tens of thousands of smiling German troops enjoyed billets in Austrian cities and towns until April 1945.

---

[13] Connection

Later in my life, and to my horror, I learnt almost a million of my fellow countrymen fought under their banners, including the notorious Second SS Panzer Division Das Reich, one of the last Nazi legions to depart Vienna.

But, as Leo and I travelled westward, and onward to England, we remained oblivious to these fateful events, and blind to the destiny of my mother, father and brother.

6 How Great Thou Art

When through the woods and forest glades I wander,
and hear the birds sing sweetly in the trees.
When I look down from lofty mountain grandeur
and see the brook and feel the gentle breeze.
– from "How Great Thou Art", translated from the German
by Stuart K. Hine

I sat on an old school bench in an office of the Immigration Detention Centre in La Perouse. I could barely recall meeting with Ashton Frost months earlier in the Caledonian Club in Belgravia Square. Despite denying women membership, a table in a nook behind a screen, secured for a few shillings, allowed for an intimate conversation. And yet I remember the menu: cream of asparagus soup and roast sweet potatoes with carrot for the Shetland smoked salmon, served with a garnish of crisped capers. I had not eaten during my fortnight's remand, and my ribs poked through my blouse.

A chastened Ashton attempted to explain the reason for my incarceration during a twilight drive from Long Bay Jail.

'Australia can't keep up with the edicts coming out of Canberra,' he said. 'The war is changing every aspect of our life. Enemy aliens might infiltrate the country, so one cannot be too cautious. This is why the authorities took their time checking your papers. They spent hours quizzing me about your contract.' He slapped the steering wheel in disgust.

The previous day, a po-faced turnkey supervised the delivery of my luggage. The feel of my possessions elevated my spirits from depression to sluggish torpor, a sensation not unlike the inedible glutinous stew served for dinner in the internment camp's canteen.

Ashton drove, steering his soft leather-seated Humber through a fly-blown landscape reminiscent of scenes from a Tom Mix western. Packs of slavering dogs, roaming dimly lit grimy alleys, bared their fangs and chased the car with a manic determination to shred its tyres.

We pulled into a Victorian-style rail station around midnight and boarded a private, first-class sleeping car. Porters unloaded my luggage and stowed it in a van at the rear of the train.

'We are travelling with a group of friends tonight. When you have freshened up, we would love to see you for a late supper,' Ashton said.

'Of course, Mr Frost,' I replied. 'I look forward to rekindling our acquaintance.' But after snibbing the door I lay on the bunk and sobbed into a deep sleep and slept through an insistent rat-a-tat-tat, oblivious to Ashton calling out my name.

Before dawn a porter carrying a tray of English breakfast goodies entered my cabin and roused me from exhausted sleep.

'Where are we?'

'The Blue Mountains, Miss. You alight in Medlow Bath in twenty minutes. The train continues to Bathurst, where we change crew. Enjoy your breakfast.'

Heaped sugar mellowed the strong hot tea. Hard butter melted into crispy toast and oozed into a mix of tangy orange marmalade. Scrambled eggs and bacon, and more toast and tea, then with a lick of the plate, a satisfied burp, and a familiar need to go, the miserable chain of yesterdays ended as a brilliant sun welcomed a new day.

'We missed you last night, Miss Lieder.'

'Call me Susan, or ZaSu.'

'ZaSu it is, and I am Ashton.'

***

I shivered on the platform. As the reek of burnt coal dissipated behind the disappearing steam train, I noticed an unknown fragrance perfume the cool air. Large white birds, heads bedecked with bright yellow combs, squawked and strutted on the tarmac around my feet. A squadron of multi-hued green, red and azure parrots swooped above, chattering with each other. Black and white magpies warbled a fluty carol, pecking at insects and shuffling in and out of the warming shadows.

Beyond the station, teams of workers geed bullock drays toward a grand stone entranceway, guarding a sequence of ornate structures perched on a cliff overlooking an endless valley.

'What are these buildings?'

'They're known as Foy's Folly,' Ashton said, warming his hands in the sweet dawn air.

'This vista reminds me of Lake Hallstatt,' I said, but my words triggered pangs of homesickness, and the bluish misty vista reinforced my sense of being a foreigner in an alien land.

The noise of the unloading of the two freight rail cars broke my reverie. Workers edged the Humber saloon down a ramp and onto the roadway. Next came large travelling chests, including my belongings, stout bureaux, slatted wooden crates, animal carcasses and chattels, stacked into a convoy of lorries, parked opposite the building complex Ashton called the Hydro Majestic. Local provedores from the nearby Megalong Valley offloaded produce and haggled a sales price with the Frost retinue for their excess stock.

'Why Foy's Folly?'

Ashton laughed. 'Mark built it as a mineral bath, but to my knowledge no-one has found a mineral spring, and if one exists, it probably dried up ages ago along with the Foy fortune. There is a Turkish bath on the Wynne Estate near our summer house. Health resorts were a big craze after the First World War. I've heard a rumour the Australian Army might commandeer this entire complex, but enough talk of war. Are you ready for the last part of the journey?'

'Yes, of course, but I am curious about our destination.'

'My family's summer chalet Breffni is in Mount Wilson. Sydney is unpleasant at this time of year. We'll stay for six weeks and get you settled after that nasty incident in Long Bay. Apart from Blackheath and Mount Victoria, there are no large towns for miles. We haul in all our supplies, including the fresh fruit and vegetables they are loading now. There is a waterfall on the property boundary, an everlasting spring, and a bore, but everything else comes by truck off the trains, either from here at Medlow or the Mount Wilson station near Bell.'

'Ashton, what is this sweet odour?'

'Eucalyptus gum. An essential oil found in different species of trees across Australia. The oil evaporates in the heat and tinges the air, hence the name the Blue Mountains. I don't notice it these days unless a logging dray passes. The smell can be overpowering, and the oil is flammable. If a forest of gum tress catch fire, and a wind gets behind the blaze, only rain will put it out.

'The Hydro survived several bushfires after the Foys started building forty-odd years ago, but the trees and shrubs grow back, as if nothing happened,' Ashton said, taking his foot off the clutch and slipping the saloon into gear. 'Off we go.'

But the car struggled to reach twenty miles an hour as he swerved to avoid ruts, potholes and fallen branches.

Cicadas thrummed the warming air, dulcified with scents reminiscent of honey and vanilla, cinnamon, nutmeg and anise. An olfactory melange swirled from trees. Shrubs, burdened with clusters of blossoms, bowed as if to snap. Flower baubles high in the passing canopy enticed birds to feed on their nectar. I imagined the screeches of the white birds with the yellow combs the mating call of a pterodactyl.

Ashton introduced Deborah Hull, his fiancé, and the man by her side, Deborah's brother, Stanley, Ashton's tennis partner.

'The men play cricket, tennis and croquet,' Ashton said.

'And we women play canasta, or billiards, or the new American game of pool. What is your favourite brand?' Deborah asked.

'Brand?'

'Cigarettes, silly. I prefer a Sobraine, or the occasional Cuban cigar, but they are so scarce.' Deborah giggled.

'I don't smoke.'

But Deborah proclaimed, 'We'll soon change that! When in the Blue Mountains you'll become a smoky mountaineer.'

A titter of laughter greeted her attempt at humour.

'I love your brooch.'

Deborah unclasped the pendant. 'Ashton had it made for me at Hancocks of London.'

'A Monarch butterfly,' Ashton said. 'There are thousands in the mountains.'

The dense scrub gave way to forests of tree ferns growing in tight groups by hairpin bends coiling around waterfalls bisecting the steep road. From within these glades, a melodious sonority replaced the toneless thrum of cicadas. Echoing single chimes became a chorus of multiple trills.

'Bellbirds,' Deborah said. 'There are hundreds in this gully.'

'And when we hear them, we're close,' Ashton said.

A stout dry-stone wall signified the presence of unseen others. Manicured grass grew to the edge of the road. Double rows of tall Canadian maples lined carriageways curving out of sight. Dark red-brick houses appeared on either side of the graded road, not unlike my family's Surrey estate. Scores of familiar trees, like those I played under as a child – birch, alder, oak and ash – replaced the wild scribbly eucalyptus, their attendant parrots, and laughing kingfishers called kookaburra. Pink cherries, plane trees, lime, almond, elm, chestnut, beech, apple, liquidambar and species I did not know formed dappled avenue entrances to the barely glimpsed estates. Haughty peacocks strolled and squawked alarms amidst manicured groves.

'How beautiful,' I said, as Ashton steered the car between two enormous wrought-iron gates adorned with the family crest.

On first view the lines of the Frost house seemed different from the neighbouring estates, glimpsed on the inbound drive.

After alighting and stretching the cramps from my stiff muscles, I recognised the architectural praxis.

'Prairie School.'

'Take a bow, Miss Lieder,' Ashton said, placing an arm my shoulder.

'Frank Lloyd Wright?'

'Close,' Ashton said.

A servant welcomed us to Breffni.

The pitched roof comprised thousands of cedar shingles. The alternating shades of brick on the tall, wide chimneys, the stained-glass windows, and the wood panelling, sang the praises of the Arts and Crafts movement.

'Who is the architect?'

'Walter Burley Griffin, an American and a colleague of Frank Lloyd Wright. Bit of an odd bod, if you ask me, what with his vegetarianism and what have you. Designed our capital city, Canberra, and an inland town called Griffith.'

'Is Griffith near a town called Hay?' I kept the tone of my voice neutral.

'I think so, but why so curious?' Ashton asked, escorting me to the rear of the estate.

'A man I met aboard ship said he came from Hay, and I thought it peculiar to give a town an agricultural name.'

'To be honest, I am not sure which large town is nearby, but I will tell you if I find out,' Ashton said, and switched the conversation back to Burley Griffin.

'Walter showed me diagrams of houses he designed for Wright's clients in Denver, Colorado,' he said. 'Griffin's houses are a perfect fit for Australia, and this one,' he added with a sweep of his arm, 'is ideal for this climate.

'We get winter snow, so big open fires and snug bedrooms are just the ticket,' he continued, as we walked across a lawn cultivated with alternating species of grass which sloped toward the lip of a gully. 'It's a pity you won't get to meet Walter. He died after a nasty fall during a jaunt to India… time for lunch.'

'I am famished,' I said.

'So am I.'

We walked arm in arm to a coolly decorated dining room; a setting for twenty senior Frost staff and close family friends adorned an ovate wooden table.

'You'll forget everyone's name after a sherry or four.' Ashton smiled as a beaming Deborah signalled the staff to serve the jugged hare, marinated and cooked in red wine with juniper berries and served with a sauce made from the animal's liver, diced mushrooms, and combined with heavy cream. Mashed potatoes and green beans steamed beneath finely wrought silver food cloches.

'Before we begin this first of many happy summer meals,' Ashton said, 'please stand for the loyal toast.'

The guests raised their drinks toward a portrait of King George VI and sang the opening chorus of the national anthem.

As the rondo reached its climax, Ashton said, 'God save the King.' The assembled company repeated the sentiment in unison. 'A hearty appetite everyone, and please welcome ZaSu to our merry band,' Ashton added.

Tinkling crystal clinked assent to Ashton's toast. I bowed and said, 'Thank you,' and sat next to Deborah.

'I'm so happy you are with us in Australia,' said Deborah, calling the waiter to bring a carafe.

'When are you to be married?'

After swallowing a mouthful of claret, Deborah warmed to the topic and spoke of arrangements for an autumn nuptial. 'I am worried about this dreadful war. I am certain Ashton will join up, and if his father is anything to go by, he will insist Ashton serve on the front line. Jeremiah and Cornelia arrive tomorrow. Trust me, he will bore you silly with tales of derring-do on the Western Front.' Deborah sighed after her fifth swallow of wine. 'Not that I doubt his bravery. But I simply cannot abide the idea of being separated from Ashton.'

Dessert of blancmange followed by tea and biscuits, and sherry after sherry, mellowed the stiff beginning to the meal. Guests turned face-on, repeating this or that anecdote about the Frost empire, and laughed at off-colour jokes.

I touched Deborah's hand and asked, 'Who have you commissioned to design your wedding gown?'

Deborah beamed, delighted at being the focus of our conversation.

'I've looked at so many catalogues, but I do not know where to begin,' she said through a sherry haze.

I pounced on her momentary lapse of confidence. 'I would consider it an honour to create your gown and your bridesmaids' ensembles.'

Deborah's mouth formed a silent 'Oh'.

'Your dress will be the initial Creation by ZaSu for the Frost Emporium.'

I asked for drawing materials, and, on a cleared space on the table, with a pencil in each hand, I sketched two consummate but distinct outlines of wedding gowns, showing trains, veils and shoes. Minutes passed in silence as a knot of guests watched my artworks unfold. I signed my name at the bottom of each sketch and presented Deborah with the drawings.

'We had nothing like this at Frensham,' she said, calling for Ashton to examine the folios, but the interim head of the house had stepped out to the tennis court with Deborah's brother, Stanley.

'Where did you study?' Deborah asked, glancing about in search of Ashton.

'I did not go to a school. We had tutors for classes in mathematics, geography, fine art, language and fencing.'

'You fence?'

'*En garde,*' I said, with a stylised flourish of a silver spoon.

'And what languages do you speak?'

'Hungarian, French, Czech, German, Polish and Romanian, which I think is similar to Portuguese and English. And what did you study, Deborah?'

'I graduated deportment for the debutante's ball. A little home economics, needlework and French. I was not good at arithmetic. Besides, a girl needs to marry the man of her dreams, and your gown will make my dreams come true,' she said in a tipsy, singsong voice. 'But you, my dear, are about to become a Blue Mountaineer.'

Deborah removed two Sobraine cigarettes from a gold case.

'No argument. Put this between your lips and breathe in when I light the tip,' she said, clicking twice on a gold lighter.

My head spun. I coughed and spluttered a lungful of smoke into Deborah's laughing face. The burning nicotine triggered a queasy sensation.

A guest shouted, 'She's going to barf, look out.'

I ran to the rear of the house, out the door, and deposited the meal plus wine onto a freshly dressed rose bed. Nausea returned a second and third time, but as the fuzziness cleared, I looked up and saw Ashton break free from Stanley's flamboyant embrace.

'Are you all right?' Ashton asked. 'Never mind the mess. The gardener will rake it over.'

Gulps of fresh air helped calm my urge to regurgitate again.

'My first and last cigarette,' I said.

'Let me guess: one of Deborah's stinky Sobraines. What you just saw—'

I cut Ashton short. 'Men embrace and kiss one another

in every village and city across Europe. I saw two men being affectionate, nothing more. No need to explain, dear Ashton. I am the one who made a fool of herself, but please, do not betray Deborah.'

Stanley caught up, and when Ashton slipped out of sight for an instant, I mimed a puckered kiss in his direction. In return, Stanley placed his lips to fingers and sent a slight blow of air toward me. With this reciprocal gesture, I knew I had made a friend.

The evening rolled on with cricket on the lawn, while indoors, billiards and card games descended into comic farce thanks to wine and whiskey.

By midnight I declared time for bed, but, as Ashton bid me good night, Stanley remarked, 'Don't be too late tomorrow morning. I am taking us for a walk.'

Stanley meant eight o'clock on Sunday morning, far too early, save for guests with his athletic stamina.

***

Stanley retrieved a breakfast tray from a servant and tapped on my door.

'Go away,' I said, but Stanley insisted I greet the day.

'Up and at 'em,' he said.

'Coffee. Please. Coffee.'

Stanley called the waiter while I stormed about, seeking suitable clothes.

'I'll eat when we get back from wherever it is you are taking me,' I said.

'Sensible shoes, dear,' Stanley cautioned, as we passed through the rear door next to the scene of my nocturnal embarrassment.

'Meet Wiley, our head gardener,' Stanley said, and pointing toward a russet-coloured dog, continued, 'Say hello to Gingie, but I do not recommend patting him.'

Wiley pulled a heavy haversack on to his back and Stanley placed an outsized slouch hat on my head.

The steep track, like the road driven yesterday, curved around sharp hairpins. I lost my sense of direction within twenty minutes. Gingie, sniffing and raising a leg at every tree fern, darted among bushes and bracken. No-one spoke. The clammy air grew cool the deeper we climbed down the side of the mountain. The wide sky disappeared. Towering ferns robbed the competing undergrowth of light. The whiff of humus smelt of fungus and rotting vegetation. Bellbirds chimed. An unseen animal, wary of Gingie's restless scratching, bolted into a redoubt. A whipbird cracked the silence. Down, spiralling down, then with a raised hand, Wiley stopped and pointed. A small, motionless bird stood on the track ahead. A faint whistle brought Gingie to a halt. Mimicking the tone of Wiley's trill, the bird displayed a fan of silky feathers.

'A male lyrebird after a mate,' Wiley whispered, as the bird unleashed a torrent of sounds, identical to the noises we had made on our downward trek.

We paused in a dell bathed in dappled light and festooned with flowering bushes. Wiley pulled at a bunch of fruit, ate a handful, and offered another bunch to me and Stanley.

'This lot's sweet,' he said. Stanley's eyes brightened as he bit into the lilly pilly, but I hesitated.

'Go on take a bite, Miss. Slakes the thirst, and it's good for your skin.'

I swallowed the nectar.

The roar of water filled the air. A prismatic hue hovered above a deep rock pool. Swirls of Monarch butterflies sipped from small, shallow depressions. The chill air laved my senses and our laughing, swimming voices echoed in the canyon. Gingie howled.

'Can't stay long,' Wiley said, sparking a fire of eucalyptus-scented leaves and twigs stacked between river rocks. 'Harder going up than down, eh? The heat will help youse dry off. There's kangaroo and wallaby 'ere and maybe wombat up in those cliffs.' Then he passed out thick cut sandwiches.

A spikey echidna ignored Gingie's nosey snout and continued digging among the leaf litter. A wedge-tailed eagle circled overhead.

'Any platypus in this pond?' Stanley asked Wiley.

'Yes, and a feed of yabbies, but, when you get dry, make sure you check your feet for leeches. You won't feel 'em, but don't worry, I've got salt.'

Tiny, worm-like creatures wriggled on my ankles.

'Get them off me.'

The suckers shrivelled and fell to the ground with a touch of the grains of salt, but a thin stream of blood stained my flesh and dripped into the dirt.

'Lilly pilly juice will fix you up. You'll be as right as rain.'

'Better go. We can't be late for vespers,' Stanley said.

With a mischievous twinkle, Wiley described rock python, copperhead snakes, redback spiders, ticks, mosquitoes, funnel webs and other unseen denizens of the scrub.

'Stop scaring her,' Stanley said, but Gingie's threatening growl put Stanley in his place.

'Sing out if you get tired, Miss, and I'll carry ya,' Wiley said.

Gingie leapt and scampered toward an exposed butte, which glowed gold in the sun.

***

The outdoor assembly for evensong banished last night's jovial mood. Starched collars and heavy grey suits transformed the male house guests from yesterday's freewheeling band. Ankle-length plain frocks, long-sleeved gloves and modest headwear transformed otherwise vivacious women into dowdy frumps.

Unnoticed, Stanley and I snuck into the back row. Deborah coiled away from the Ashton family, arrayed in the front, stood next to me, took my arm and whispered, 'Just in time for Sabbath prayers.'

'Sabbath was yesterday,' I said.

'No, it wasn't. It's Sunday, silly. Where have you been?'

'I've mixed up my days with all this travelling.'

As the congregation sang the opening stanza of the hymn "How Great Thou Art", Deborah took my hand and whispered an altered lyric, 'How great your art,' but I slipped from her grip, and turned away from the puzzled bride-to-be.

No matter the gravity of the occasion, I could not abide listening to this version of a popular tune written by the Swedish preacher Carl Boberg, stolen by the Nazis and used as Germany's national marching song. Each day with fanatical gusto, millions of Nazis sang the words *Die Fahne Hoch*[14] in praise of the dead Sturmführer Horst Wessel, formerly of Berlin's Sturmabteilung.[15]

---

[14] raise the flag
[15] stormtroopers

7 Hay

> We'll make the tyrants feel the sting
> o' those that they would throttle;
> they needn't say the fault is ours
> if blood should stain the wattle.
>
> – from Henry Lawson's poem "Freedom on the Wallaby"

As a boxer, Leo knew a parry is only effective if muscles are strong enough to withstand repeated blows, so, if a haematoma is inevitable, better to coil into a tight ball and protect the head and vital organs.

Leo chose the biggest of the men bashing him – the leader – and saved strength for a retaliatory strike. He aimed for the philtrum, the groove in the middle of the upper lip. If timed properly, a blow with the heel of the hand should knock out two front teeth and smash the septum into the skull, resulting in a spectacular haemorrhage.

The subsequent beating which followed his retaliation against the boss of the internment guards at Sydney's Central Rail Station left Leo semiconscious during the ensuing twenty-hour train journey.

Odd sounding names – Junee, Coolamon, Grong Grong, Narrandera, Yanco, and other Wiradjuri and Nari Nari words – peppered the guards' conversations. Each lurching stop/start ticked off a milestone toward the one English word Leo recognised. Hay.

A hobnailed boot slammed into his upper thigh.

'The country's full of these dagos.'

'Na, he's a German.'

'No, he's not, you idiot.'

'His papers say he is a zeck-oh-slo something or other. I can't pronounce these wog words.'

45

Bringagee, Groongal, Carrathool, Uardry, Beabula.

'Hay's next stop, boys.'

'Thank Christ.'

'Get up, you wuss.'

Leo stood.

***

In a late evening gathering at a campfire, a guard, sporting a mouse-sized swelling under a crimson eye, reckoned he saw more whirling galaxies than all the stars painted on the stage curtain of the Tivoli Theatre, after Leo's king hit landed square on the side of his face.

From that day on guards at the Hay Internment Camp held truncheons when they approached Leo. None came within cooee of his fists.

Aside from supervising the routine of wake-up, sick parade, breakfast and daily work details, the under-worked guards, outnumbered by inmates, relied on strands of rusting barbed wire stretched across rickety frames for the camp's security. But despite this next-to-useless fencing, inmates faced a diabolical dilemma. If someone decided to escape – easy enough to do – where would they go?

And the enticement of additional rations encouraged scores of inmates to volunteer for extra work. A chronic shortage of skilled tradespeople provided Leo with the freedom to labour on new barracks and mess halls.

Italian prisoners dominated the bricklaying and concreting gangs, but, best of all, they could cook. Within weeks, the robust flavours of basil, garlic and tomatoes added palatability to the mutton served morning, noon and night. Mutton with black tea simmered in a billy, and greasy mutton smeared on dry damper for lunch.

'Mutton and Jeff,' said the Italians, laughing at the guards who shared copies of the American cartoon characters.

Truckloads of old wethers bleated their last at an impromptu abattoir, built a half a mile from the encampment boundary. The Italians volunteered for slaughterhouse work and brought the best of the offal back to the camp for Sunday cookouts of sweet breads, diced liver and sizzling kidneys, tossed with roasted garlic and served with a tomato dressing.

Musical instruments made from bits of cadged wood and catgut strings lightened the nightly monotony. Chess tournaments thrived. Impromptu choirs sang for everyone. And still the detainees arrived; trainloads of bewildered Europeans destined to consume huge vats of mutton stew.

After a heavy night on the grog, the guards slept in on Saturdays and ignored the detainees for the rest of the day. On weekends, graziers with their wives and families came into town for a matinee at the pictures, or a dance at the back of the pub.

Hay's cafés served numerous plates of steak and eggs, fried tomato and mushrooms with white bread and butter, toasted or plain, on the side. Pots of tea with rock cakes and strawberry jam, followed by sago pudding or trifle, served as dessert. No such fare for the detainees. One of the new arrivals, shipped from London aboard the *HMT Dunera*, supervised a dish of liver served with parsley, garlic and fried potatoes. Not to be outdone, an Italian cook made pasta melded with sweetbread and tripe in a dish he called *pajata alla finta*. After a round of applause, he announced his next project, *vino rosso*, but obtaining a grapevine cutting might prove difficult.

'Mr Leo, if you see one on your travels, please,' he said.

As part of his duties, Leo travelled to the Murrumbidgee River to wait at a wharf for barges loaded with lumber shipped from South Australia.

A local man who passed the time with Leo told the story of Burke and Wills, who in the preceding century crossed the near empty Murrumbidgee at this point on their slow trudge to an ignoble death.

In the town of Balranald, Leo learnt about the horror of drought, a phenomenon he had never experienced in Europe. Tens of thousands of excellent quality sheep, bearing superb fleece and waiting to be shorn, dropped dead from the unbearable heat. Yet the wild animals – mysterious kangaroo and fleet of foot emu – seemed impervious to the hellish temperatures.

A labour shortage plagued the entire district. Local shearers ensured their comrades worked, but soon hundreds and then thousands of workers refused to shear the Merino, choosing to walk or catch a train to Yanco or the nearest recruiting depot to enlist in the armed forces instead.

Older men and women predominated in the villages and settlements Leo passed during the return trip to Hay. And though he had no experience with shearing, a lifetime of sorting and grading a range of animal skins seemed a tradeable sideline.

The workforce shortage worried senior bureaucrats in far off Canberra as Australia transitioned from peace to wartime. And while the armed services swelled with willing, able-bodied men, the owners of big rural stations watched their cloven-hooved fortunes shrivel and die.

An amnesty of sorts meant suitable enemy aliens could sign up to work on properties surrounding Hay.

Leo's Italian acquaintance said the local ladies he met on these week-long outings enjoyed the jiggy jig, his term for sex.

When the war finished, he said, he would marry a local girl, buy land, and grow oranges and olives along the floodplains.

'Don't you miss Italy?' Leo asked.

'No. Europe is finished. I can buy thousands of acres here and grow whatever I want. You should do the same, Mr Leo. You are a healthy man with your whole life in front of you. Why not stay here? It's good. Hard, but these are fine people.' He paused and chewed on a blade of grass. 'No-one bothers you. In Europe, everybody wants to know what you are doing. Here,' he said, sweeping an arm over the expanse of the Hay Plain, 'no nosey parker.'

He told Leo he had learnt this phrase from a girl he was secretly courting. Her father, he said, would shoot him if he found out.

'But I teach her how we both keep safe. I am born in Padua,' he said with a wink, 'and our neighbours are the Gozzi family who looked after my hero from a long time ago. You know who I am talking about?'

Leo shrugged. 'No idea.'

'Giacomo Casanova,' he said, holding his thumb and two fingers for an emphatic kiss on his lips.

Leo laughed and said, 'I will get your vine cutting. I promise.'

To the displeasure of the squattocracy, the ever-expanding internment camp sucked up quantities of scarce resources. Graziers complained to the local mayor that the lazy so-and-so's bludging off King and Country should get off their arses and earn their keep. In response, the Italians organised tennis tournaments and bocce competitions and made rude gestures at onlookers standing near the barbed wire fence. In turn the rubberneckers shouted abuse at the inmates, whom they believed lived in a holiday camp.

The term jiggy jig, accompanied by a crude gesture for sexual intercourse, gained snickering popularity among adolescent cow cockies, as rumours of domestic bashings became popular bar talk.

The camp's skilled plasterers, bricklayers, carpenters, and tailors passed their leisure hours studying at an unofficial university, reading an in-house newspaper, listening to Bach and Beethoven, or losing small fortunes of their own minted currency during all night card games of *Briscola*.

The citizens of Hay had no inkling that artists, philosophers, economists, composers, physicists and engineers lived in their midst. For the bulk of the citizenry, these people were nothing but reffos.

Leo, who learnt Australian rather than English, heard the phrase, 'make the most of the opportunity'. How could he do anything different? He mimicked common local parlance including bluey or mate, cobber, cove, digger, ratbag, bludger, ganger, cocky, boss cocky, and squatter. And he learnt terrible descriptions of Indigenous and Chinese people, the worst reserved for women, but of all these new expressions swirling as clouds of flies across his face, one proved a rip snorter. Union. In Hay, union meant the shearers, and Leo planned to make their acquaintance.

His introduction to a social class known as the rural squattocracy came days after a skyward hand approved him as a volunteer to work on a new shearing shed. The distance from the encampment meant an extended billet, plus pay and supplies.

At first, Leo confused the word swag for portable bedding until a stockman told him the term meant sundry supplies or goods packed into a bluey and humped on the back. If the station's boss cocky approved swag, they were in for a long trek on foot.

The work gang would build the shearing shed, a day's walk from the station, or mansion, owned and operated by the grazier. A bullock dray carted wood and building supplies. The temperature: one hundred degrees Fahrenheit.

A gathering held the night before the morning departure to the building site revealed the social divide in operation on this private property larger than Belgium.

The station owner rode up to the men, introduced the overseer, remounted his horse, and rode back to the distant mansion. Leo never saw the man again.

The overseer pointed out latrines, a mess hall, the supply shed for drawing swag, water tanks, a shower block, sleeping shed, and campfire. He told the men to avoid the young black women employed to fetch and carry under the supervision of an elderly matron.

'I'll put a bullet in ya if you go near 'em, or worse, you'll cop a spear in the thigh. Understand?'

An unseen worker said, 'And I thought they were flamin' orphans!'

'Youse all know Noel from the Australian Workers Union. You will be paid according to set rates, except the reffos.'

'They get the same rates as all of us, Graham,' Noel said, pointing at the internment camp inmates.

'But they're volunteers, Noel, not Australians.'

'And they are white men and workers, and when I sign 'em up they are union members, so they are treated like everyone else, Graham. Understand?'

Silence in the shed.

'I'm not joking, Graham.'

'Righto. I'll take it up with the boss.'

'You do that. He loves the feel of your tongue up his arse.'

'Fuck off, Noel.'

Laughter rippled the ranks of the Indigenous women. A girl who said 'shame job' felt the matron's cane on the back of her legs.

'Smoko,' Noel said.

'What about our tucker, Noel?'

'Let's have a rollie and a chat first, then we'll get into it.'

Noel waved to Leo to join him.

'I understand you're good with your fists, mate.'

Leo shrugged, nodded, and said, 'When I have to be.'

'And you want to become a shearer.'

'Yeah, I do, and you're the man to talk with.'

'In a manner of speaking, but...'

'But what'? Leo replied.

'Fight me for it, and if I like the way you handle yourself, I'll tell you.'

Noel double-clicked his tongue and winked. A texture reminiscent of knotted ironbark covering the skin of an anvil-weighted hand rested on Leo's shoulder.

'You reckon you can take me, cobber?'

'My oath, comrade,' Leo said.

'On ya, mate.'

The men walked to the mess hall, sat at a bench, and spooned into steaming mutton stew, discoloured with dollops of green pea mush.

Noel shouted at the assembled work crew. 'This is bloody fart fodder.'

Years would pass before I learnt these details of Leo's life in the Hay Internment Camp, courtesy of a gruff, rough and ready man named Noel O'Grady.

8 A universal provider

Of all my associates within the Frost enterprise, Deborah Hull became an ally and a friend. I think she considered me an outsider, and therefore not a threat to her relationship with Ashton. On the verge of changing her name to Frost by marriage, Deborah described the history of the family she was about to join. To understand the Frosts, Deborah said, I had to learn about the motivations of their founder.

Over a long, lazy Sydney Sunday afternoon, as Ashton prepared to join his regiment, Deborah described how decades of draughty Presbyterianism had moulded the Frost patriarch. Jeremiah Frost, she said, was known as 'the great hater'.

'His friends reckon Jeremiah would haggle the last farthing from the price of his coffin and insist the undertaker place the first sixpence he'd earned, into his dead, bony hand.'

This frugality, coupled with a canny business sense, prompted Jeremiah to establish one of Australia's largest mercantile chains. Affectionately known as Frosties, the emporium sourced, supplied and sold practical, well-made products of every description.

According to Deborah, Jeremiah borrowed the motto of an English city – 'from a needle to an anchor' – as the emporium's catchphrase.

With a canny sense of what customers needed rather than what they desired, Jeremiah invested profits in up-and-coming enterprises, including those whose products had ready markets in booming rural towns and cities. Frost emporiums sold ornate pressed metal sheeting, woollen carpets and school uniforms. And, as a matter of honour, Jeremiah listed outstanding local and British innovations in the store catalogue.

Though a loyal subject of the King, Jeremiah esteemed the work and aspirations of fellow Presbyterian John Dunmore Lang, whose mistrust of colonial governors and advocacy of republicanism set Lang apart from conservative political orthodoxy.

The elder Frost detested the British banker Otto Niemeyer, who in the early 1930s sneered at Australian optimism while demanding the people accept a lower standard of living. Old man Frost wrongly derided Niemeyer as a Jew.

But Jeremiah's colleagues argued the merits of Niemeyer's call for deflation, and the popular sentiment of unleashing Australia's potential by spending the nation out of a long economic slump.

The teetotaller Jeremiah, however, believed in the primacy of an Australian central bank over the Bank of England. According to Deborah, Jeremiah said when cash flowed free of British interference, the nation glowed.

The old man declared his son, Deborah's fiancé Ashton, would inherit Lang's progressive aspirations. As a youth standing at his father's side on the shop floor of the Frost headquarters on Oxford Street in Sydney, Ashton learnt a basic truth: women browse before purchasing, whereas men buy what they need and exit. And though the men earned the money, most fidgeted, and shifted from foot to foot, watching the cash pass through the hands of their wives, daughters or sisters.

'Women are Frosties' customers of choice,' Deborah said, 'and Ashton decreed all display windows and shop interiors be decorated to attract female customers. Most of the cashiers are women, as are its best floorwalkers.'

Female customers parked their husbands in the basement next to bulky stock, so Jeremiah ordered the shop barbers set up their chairs on the lower floors alongside tobacconists and suit salesmen. And the nearby popular cafeteria stocked and sold breakfast and lunch selections, familiar on domestic dinner tables. Customers queued for scones baked with the secret ingredient of lemon soda, which imparted a faint fizz and tang: perfect with a pot of Robur Tea, fresh strawberry jam and whipped cream.

Frosties bustled. From top floor management suites to hordes of storemen and packers running the cellars, the enterprise hummed to the sound of swishing vacuum tubes, sucking cash, invoices and memos along its mercantile arteries.

'Meet you at Frosties' became a weekend clarion for the start of a Sydney Saturday outing. Ashton instructed the in-house advertising agency to add the slogan to Frost's promotional materials, which featured a smiling female face.

'And I'm the lass with the smiling face,' Deborah said with an embarrassed laugh.

Each morning while strolling the shop's departments, Jeremiah reminded staff to mind the pennies, for the pounds would take care of themselves.

Father and son understood a simple fact. Wages paid to women in their employ put food on tables, and a modest Christmas bonus made for loyal staff, who remained with the emporium throughout their working lives.

Young Mister Frost, as he was known among his father's circle, noticed wealthy matrons from Sydney's leafy suburbs spent their spare cash on luxuries. The Great Depression gradually released its grip on the country, and with the return of prosperity, thanks to strong prices for wool and wheat, these wives and mothers demanded items redolent of the good life. Shoes, dresses, stylish undergarments, perfume, soap, makeup, hats and gloves, handbags, cigarette lighters and jewellery, snapped up as soon as display items reached the shelves. During buying trips to London, Ashton also noticed the daughters and wives of the British middle class spent fortunes on haute couture, and the finest examples came from Continental design houses.

'And this is where you come in, dearest ZaSu,' Ashton had said, determined to secure the best of these creations.

'The designs by the House of Liebler are the finest in Europe, and affordable,' Deborah said.

Although the Wall Street Crash crippled the world's economy, Ashton had heeded the impact of the creative energy unleashed during the Roaring Twenties. Despite the havoc of the global economic collapse, the automation which boomed courtesy of an unregulated stream of capital, spelt the end of the Victorian era across the British Empire, except Australia.

'Ashton has plans to expand the family interests in the way aviation, the telegram, and the telephone shrank the globe,' she added. 'He reckons European flair, British quality and American mass production techniques require innovation, design and technology. And I trust his judgement. To be the undisputed universal provider of the future, Frosties must embrace new ways of trading, and ignore the likes of Otto Niemeyer.'

Deborah said Ashton introduced a Frost-branded credit card, as well as lay-bys to ensure store loyalty. Hard-working consumers who could prove financial security were encouraged to join a store loyalty program, which meant Frosties continued to clothe, furnish and sustain generations of purchasers.

'And he believes in the idea of welcoming the world's best and brightest,' Deborah went on. 'He reckons this is in Australia's best interests and it's why he worked so hard to bring you to Sydney. He said you are the first of many creative thinkers from overseas who'll give Frosties a competitive edge.'

'But surely there are designers in Sydney as good as me,' I replied.

'Of course,' Deborah said, 'and they are snapped up by our competitors. It's a cutthroat business, and I'm sure it is the same in Austria, and it certainly is in England. The problem for Australia is our miniscule population, and this is one point where father and son disagree.'

Deborah said Jeremiah endorsed the philosophy of Australia's delegate to the failed Evian Conference on Refugees, Colonel T. W. White, who proclaimed, 'As we have no real racial problem, we are not desirous of importing one, by encouraging any scheme of large-scale foreign migration.'

I told Deborah that I was one of a handful of Europeans who came to Australia and benefitted from a wealthy man's vision of a creative, enterprising nation. But, from the time of my arrival, I had decided to say nothing about the unstoppable rise of fanatical militarism financed by the unfettered flow of capital in western Europe, and the dead hand of five-year plans in the USSR. I feared if I said too much, I would draw unwelcome attention to my identity and jeopardise my right to remain in Australia. Deportation meant my certain death.

And as war throttled Europe, neither Ashton, Jeremiah nor most Australians realised the unthinkable was occurring in real time. As the sun set on the British Empire, a Rising Sun shone to the north. Fifty-six million Japanese citizens pledged allegiance to an emperor, who ruled from a throne decorated with stylised Chinese chrysanthemums.

9 Z Weave

I telephoned Deborah for advice about my first formal meeting with the senior Frost management in the emporium's headquarters.

'Jeremiah's a numbers man,' Deborah said. 'He prefers tweedy accountants to big talking salesmen. He will ask how you plan to broaden Frosties' appeal to female customers. Tell him you are planning a dedicated bridal salesroom in the city store, and that I am your first customer.'

'Any advice on how I should dress?'

'Twinset with pearls, matching gloves and handbag,' Deborah said. 'Jeremiah isn't comfortable dealing with women. We are supposed to do what we are told. Ashton is not like his father, thank goodness. The old man will quiz you about things you haven't dreamt of.'

'Such as?'

'Your hairstyle for starters,' Deborah said. 'I love your Louise Brooks bob, but Sydney women do not wear their hair short like you. Stick to your guns and you'll be fine. Let me know how you go.'

I recalled Ashton describing Sydney's hot, muggy summers but the mid-autumn May day of our meeting proved milder than the earlier weeks of stifling, sleepless nights on a hard mattress in a boarding house in Kings Cross.

I set off by tram to Hyde Park and the short walk to Frosties. The atmosphere in Jeremiah's office proved as chilly as one of his high-minded talks.

'Please take a seat, Miss Lieder. How do you take your tea? Milk and sugar?'

Ashton remained silent, face pale, lips bloodless.

'May I have black coffee, please?'

Jeremiah's bushy raised eyebrows signalled surprise, but he rang a bell on his desk and told his assistant to fetch the beverage.

'We have chicory coffee, madam,' she said.

But Jeremiah interrupted, saying, 'Yes, yes, that's fine.'

Turning to me, he said, 'I'm not sure if you are aware of the news, but Sydney was attacked last night by several Japanese submarines.'

During the previous evening, dozens of police cars and fire engines, sirens blaring, raced past my boarding house, towards Potts Point. The concierge assured residents the fire, or whatever it was, would be extinguished.

'My contact in the Department of Defence in Canberra tells me a full-scale naval battle erupted in the Harbour. Dozens killed. This information is in the hands of the Government Censor to stop panic, so please, not a word to anyone. And the Japs shelled the coastline from Newcastle to the Eastern Suburbs. I am telling you this, Miss Lieder, because these events have a direct impact on this company.'

The hot chicory made me gag.

Ashton picked up the thread. 'The Frost Emporium is bound by a contract to you, but I am afraid as of now, we cannot fulfil its terms. We are at war, and this company is gazetted as an official supplier to the Department of Defence. As a result, we cannot offer you an ongoing role, commensurate with your skills.' Beads of sweat glistened on his forehead.

'What young Mister Frost is saying, Miss Lieder, is we are letting you go,' Jeremiah said.

Bile rose in my stomach.

'Please, this is not a one-way conversation.' Jeremiah tinkled the desk bell and ordered a carafe of water and the removal of the stinking chicory. 'Speak your mind.'

'I chatted with Ashton's fiancé last night,' I said. 'We discussed the upcoming wedding. Deborah suggested I mention the possibility of designing an in-store bridal suite. I am afraid this is the only thing I can contribute. Like you, I am shocked by last night's news.'

My idea of allocating a floor dedicated to weddings lightened the mood.

Jeremiah tinkled the bell a second time and called for 'Real coffee for Miss Lieder, not that awful chicory stuff. You realise Young Mister Frost is joining the Second Imperial Force, the AIF, as a commissioned officer.'

'Deborah mentioned this as a possibility,' I said.

'With last night's attack, and Americans arriving en masse, I begin my Army commission at the end of the week, but this still does not resolve your dilemma.'

Jeremiah dipped a biscuit into his tea.

'Iced VoVo with your coffee, Miss Lieder?'

I declined and sipped the steaming beverage.

'As of now,' Jeremiah went on, 'this company is deemed an integral part of national mobilisation. I have been directed to write to the Department of Defence, outlining our plans to contribute to the war effort. If the DoD rejects these suggestions, we could be nationalised, and our staff seconded to serve on war industries elsewhere. Australian men and women are expected to do their duty for the nation, and this includes you, Miss Lieder. Though I am reluctant to let you go, be prepared to work for the defence of the country. No-one is exempt,' Jeremiah added, dipping a second biscuit into his tea.

'And should women do their duty?'

'I expect so. As nurses and what have you.'

'Or in auxiliary military roles?'

Jeremiah looked up from his tea. 'Those types of changes started at the end of the first war, so yes, it is a possibility, in support roles and God knows what else. Why? What are you thinking?'

I stood and walked to the window, looked down at the passing trams, and after a pause, turned and faced both men and said, 'These women are going to require uniforms.'

Jeremiah rang the bell.

'Ask Mr Jenkins to join us please, Muriel.'

'And you could design them, Miss Lieder?' Ashton said, clapping his hands in triumph. Jeremiah leant back in his swivel chair.

'Yes, of course. And I imagine there will be different uniforms for all branches of services, including headwear, belts, sundry accessories and summer and winter outfits.'

'Jenkins, meet Susan Lieder. Miss Lieder, Oswald Jenkins, the company's chief accountant. Ossie, I think we have found a way out of our dilemma with those Labor bastards.'

I didn't realise at the time, but I had become the Frost Emporium's first paid consultant.

The morning meeting stretched to lunch, into the afternoon, and finished at dinner in the Australia Hotel where I inspected an ornate display case in the hotel's sumptuous foyer, containing the signature of the French chanteuse Sarah Bernhardt, who in the previous century stayed in a luxurious second-floor suite, accompanied by her St Bernard, a tiny pug, and one hundred items of luggage.

I later learnt that during the war, 25,000 Australian women, all British subjects, joined and served in the Australian Women's Army Service. These women were paid two-thirds of the male wage for their service in the signal corps, ordnance, artillery and intelligence. They worked as clerks, manual labourers, on transport and equipment maintenance, drove cars and amphibious vehicles. Most wore uniforms manufactured by companies holding licences to the Frost Emporium. I suspect few women serving in the AWAS realised the capital Z woven onto the size and measurement label of their uniform indicated my design. Z for ZaSu.

A grateful Jeremiah bought me a terraced house in Commonwealth Street. I set up a studio and created and sourced raw material for manufacture. Up to war's end, I sketched bespoke uniform templates for domestic and military nurses, police, and fire brigade personnel. I devised warm, lightweight, insulated flying suits and headwear for aviators, and created jungle and desert camouflage patterns. I developed a special type of fibre interlock, woven into fire-resistant uniforms, for use aboard battleships. The United States Navy bought the rights to the stitch for its specialist firefighting crews aboard aircraft carriers. Merino wool of the fewest micron proved the secret of the fire-suppressing pattern, and the best fleece came from Hay in south-western New South Wales.

I created a new weave for pressure bandages, absorbent gauze for wounds, and all-purpose suture material, lightly treated with lanolin for battlefield surgery. Each of my innovations passed through the Frost Emporium war supply directorate, headed by Mr Ossie Jenkins, supervisor of government tenders, and witness to my signature for the *Official Secrets Act*.

Fear of a Japanese invasion caused a collapse in the value of harbourside real estate. I bought a California-style bungalow in Seaforth for several hundred pounds. Royalties from my Z Weave, as it was called, financed the purchase.

10 The man with the iron heart

The bush telegraph hummed with catastrophic news out of the Northern Territory, but somehow the guards at the Hay Internment Camp knew details of the happenings of the outside world before anyone else.

Though war was declared in 1939, Prime Minister Curtin ordered national mobilisation after the fall of Singapore. And after the bombing of Darwin and Broome, invasion seemed inevitable.

Leo heard rumours of an amnesty for able-bodied internees who volunteered to join the AIF, but his Italian friends cautioned reticence.

'What's the point, Mr Leo? You get your head shot off for what?'

But Leo reckoned serving in the army's Pioneer Corps might mean an end to constant questioning about his nationality, and he had an ally in Noel O'Grady of the Australian Workers Union.

Leo had not wasted time during internment. Noel taught him to shear the big wrinkly-skinned Merino and cautioned that this breed shore differently from crossbred animals.

'Only gun shearers are allowed anywhere near them,' Noel said. 'Have you heard the expression "rode on the sheep's back"? These beasts are the golden fleece, mate. The finer the fibre, the higher the price, and if you become a qualified classer, as well as a gun shearer, you can haggle with the stock and station agent and their clients. Top dosh gets the gun shearers, but no scab labour, ever.'

Leo worked on the sorting tables and struck up a friendship with the district wool classer. Top shearers such as Noel and the wool classers sat together at the mess. With an innate aptitude for spotting superior quality fleece, the classer and Noel encouraged Leo to study for a certificate at the local Mechanics' Institute. After war's end, a qualification plus a paid-up membership in a powerful union meant a bright future on the land. An honourable military discharge might lead to full citizenship.

But a paradox niggled at Leo's conscience. Where and how to store my family's treasure? The answer came courtesy of a representative of the Commonwealth Bank, who visited the internment camps, looking for new customers, after signing up schoolchildren to lifetime accounts. Everyone received a tin moneybox and a passbook. The internees learnt that a lifetime account with a government-owned bank could be the first step toward citizenship. The bank manager instructed new customers to deposit their savings, no matter how small. With little thought for the humble pennies and halfpennies, they joined tens of thousands of Australians in a foolproof scheme of investing in an Australian Commonwealth.

Leo chummed up with the branch's senior teller and asked if there were fees for lodging a safe deposit box to store his internment papers. With a letter from Noel attesting his character as a union member, Leo bought a sturdy metal chest with key and locked up the bullion. No-one in Hay had an inkling about the cash value of my family's belongings sitting inside the safe. Years passed before I learnt details of the last days of Leo's internment courtesy of Noel O'Grady.

Noel told me Leo planned to spend part of the gold on prime riverfront acreage and stock it with top-quality Merino, which cost three to four times more to shear. Despite having no rights under Australian law, Leo named me in his will, thus justifying spending a portion of my wealth on a phantasm. But, if his daydreams were to become reality, he had to survive the war. Despite the chronic labour shortage, Leo felt confident he, and other able-bodied men, would be called on to serve.

'Where do you think they will invade?'

'Buggered if I know, mate. Queensland, maybe?' Noel said. 'But my guess is New Guinea in the Coral Sea, and before you ask, I know sweet fuck all about the place other than Australia took it off the Germans after the first war. It's full of malaria and the locals are headhunters.'

Leo whistled.

'And if you think this place is hot, wait till you get to the tropics.'

Noel reached for his tobacco pouch, rolled a cigarette and offered the makings to Leo.

'I don't smoke, comrade, but thanks,' Leo said, plucking a stem of grass and chewing its end.

'So why volunteer to fight for this country, after everything that has happened to you?' Noel asked, cupping his hand to shield the strike of a match from the evening breeze.

'Why not? Be worth it if I can get out of here for good. I'll take my chances, and if I survive, I will be in a stronger position to plead my case to stay on after the war and make a life.'

'Don't trust the bastards,' Noel said, inhaling and flicking the ash. 'So how did you end up here?'

Leo sensed danger in the question, and though his conversational English had improved after internment, he lacked the confidence to explain the complexity of his identity and birthright.

But Noel did not wait for Leo to answer and, unprompted, described his own heritage.

'My great-grandfather came from County Clare in Ireland. Transported for nicking a cow. Lucky to escape the noose. The story goes he got a ticket of leave after serving time at Limeburners Bay, burning oyster shells to make lime. Nasty job, mate. Anyway, the old fella stayed on and settled in the Hunter Valley. I was born in Karuah, a village north of Newcastle. My mother was a local girl,' he said, drawing deeply on the now sodden cigarette. 'We've all got secrets, so don't worry, mate, I'm not going to dob you in.'

'A border can change overnight in Europe,' Leo replied, throwing the grass stalk onto the ground. 'If you live on one side of a river on a Monday, and call yourself Czech like me, by Sunday, you are German, because a little corporal decides German-speaking Czechs are not really Czechs, but German. This happened to me, because I come from the Sudetenland, which is part of the German Reich, making me a Nazi, which I am not. And here I am.'

But Leo omitted to tell Noel a London counterfeiter chose his Czech identity. He was born in the Jura region of Swabia in Germany, close to Alsace on the French border, and next to the German-speaking portion of Switzerland, and the Austrian state of Vorarlberg. He grew up in an area of Europe which would fit into one or two of the grazing properties surrounding Hay.

As they walked toward the mess hall, a deep whirring, and a sound like sticks clapping against stones, filled the air. Voices disturbed the rhythm coming from a camp, reserved for the natives who worked on the station as cooks and ringers.

'Might be a corroboree,' Noel said, 'and before you ask, it's a ceremonial get together for blackfellas. Could also be sorry business.'

'What do you mean?'

As they approached a bright, smokeless pyre, a group of men, faces and bodies painted in white ochre, shook branches in their direction, warning them to keep their distance. Leo could not see the person spinning the bullroarer but felt the pulsing thrum in his ribs.

'Poor buggers are dropping like flies because of terrible food, grog and disease. The Grim Reaper gets us all in the end, but I swear to Christ he calls in here every other week. Leave 'em to it, eh? I am starved.'

But instead of sitting down at the mess table and tucking into steaming bowls of mutton stew and white bread, a policeman ordered them to stand their ground.

'Leo Hulbert?'

'That's me. Who is asking?'

'Come along, please.'

'And who the fuck are you?' Noel demanded.

'Stay out of this, mate.'

'Are you arresting me? What is the charge?' Leo asked.

'Why? Have you done something wrong, you reffo bastard? Come with me. We can do this the hard way,' the police officer said, unbuckling his truncheon, 'or you go peacefully, and I drop you back to the camp before lights out.'

Neither man spoke during the drive to Hay.

The policeman knocked, opened the station door, and ushered Leo into a dimly lit, sparsely furnished office.

'I am Senior Constable Begg. Sit.'

'Is this about my application to join the AIF?'

But a man dressed in civilian clothes replied, 'In a manner of speaking, yes.'

The policeman slid an envelope toward Leo.

'This document is a New South Wales Police permit allowing you to travel by train to Victoria with this gentleman. Show it to police in Albury when you change trains, or any other officer you meet, civilian or military,' he said.

'You've got twenty-four hours to straighten out your affairs in Hay. Constable Warren here' – he pointed to a junior office in the corner – 'will drive you back to the camp.'

'Are you going to tell me what this is all about?' Leo demanded.

'You can ask Mr Treloar when he picks you up, but as far as this local area command is concerned, once you are in this gentleman's company, you are no longer a person of interest in the Hay Shire. Constable Warren, if you please.'

Senior Constable Begg stood and pointed to the door as the junior police officer escorted Leo to the car.

'I don't reckon you're ever going to set foot in Hay again,' he said.

'You know a lot more about what's going on than what those two blokes just said,' Leo replied.

'Of course I do. The bush telegraph knows who's gunna fart before the person even lifts a leg. Do you want some advice, pal? Write a letter of instructions and send it by registered post to the branch manager of the Commonwealth Bank. Make sure you include your passbook number and detainee identification details. He'll take care of the rest.'

'How do you know this?'

'Because this is what they tell poor bastards to do before they tighten the noose.'

Days later in Melbourne, Leo joined exiles from the Dutch East Indies, seconded to the Royal Air Force, and volunteer pilots from Australia and New Zealand aboard a US Douglas C-47 aircraft for a week-long flight to London via the old Royal Airmail route to the Cocos Islands and Johannesburg, South Africa. During the flight Nicholas Treloar, on special assignment from Australia's fledgling security intelligence organisation to the British Special Operations Executive – the SOE – sealed Leo's fate.

The SOE, he said, held an extensive dossier on Leo, detailing his tumultuous arrival in Australia. The file noted his anti-fascist beliefs, physical strength, and proficiency in European languages, including French, Italian, a smattering of Russian, German, Serbian, Czech and English.

After landing at an RAF base outside London, Leo faced two grim options. Take part in an SOE operation or spend ten years in Belmarsh prison for using forged documents during wartime. Treloar said if he accepted the assignment, all records of his transgression would disappear. Temporarily deafened during the long flight, Leo shouted agreement.

He began basic instruction at the No. 1 Parachute Training School at RAF Ringway near Manchester. Leo's mission: deliver a cache of small arms and explosives to a resistance cell. If he succeeded, he was to return to Britain, or sit out the war in Switzerland, courtesy of diplomatic papers.

'What's the destination?' he asked.

'A village outside Prague,' Treloar replied.

'I love Czech beer,' Leo said.

But what he didn't realise was that the Czechoslovak government-in-exile, based in London, had appointed Jan Kubiš and Jozef Gabčík to undertake a dangerous mission. Trained by the SOE, they had been hiding in Prague since 1941. As the time approached for their assignment, they realised their armaments and explosives were useless. Despite a cache of new Sten guns and a modified anti-tank mine supplied by Leo, the weapons failed a second time. But Kubiš and Gabčík mortally wounded their target, SS-Obergruppenführer Reinhard Heydrich,[16] a murderous Gestapo thug, and principal architect of the Holocaust. Adolph Hitler ordered the slaughter of 1,300 Czech citizens, including two hundred women, as revenge for Heydrich's death on 4 June 1942.

Nicholas Treloar had no interest in Leo Hulbert, who he deemed expendable. During the war, compromised recruits – many press-ganged from London's criminal underworld and similarly extorted – risked their lives on suicidal SOE missions.

Despite the mission's success, Leo failed to contact his London handlers and was subsequently listed as missing, presumed dead. His file was stamped, 'Sealed for a Century'.

---

[16] German author and Nobel Prize laureate Thomas Mann described Reinhard Heydrich as 'the man with the iron heart'.

11 Mata Hari's daughter?

'A Miss Deborah is on the line asking for Suze. She means you. Should I put her through?'

'How does she sound?'

'Tipsy.'

'At this hour? Pop her on please, Estelle.'

'Darling,' Deborah said, 'you need to tell your staff to hop to it. I've been waiting to speak with you for an age.'

'You're the one on the hops, Deborah. It's 9:30 in the morning, for Christ's sake!'

'Hair of the dog, dearie. Big do at the Australia Hotel last night. Nothing wrong with a Bloody Mary or two to flush the cobwebs. Lunch at Beppi's?'

'I'm in the middle of a "Looking Forward to Spring" shoot for the *Weekly*.'

'Be a darling, Suze. I need to talk to you. Make a reservation for one o'clock?'

'See you there.'

'Estelle. Clear my schedule for ninety minutes from 12:45 pm and take a message if Miss Deborah calls again.'

'Of course.'

'Which designers' work are we shooting?'

'Mr Erik, Miss Maggy Rouff and Monsieur Jacques Heim.'

'And are the models ready to go?'

'Waiting for you to call the shots.'

'We'll start with Erik's piqué weave. Set up a black background to emphasise the white rose. And do we have music for our poor, dear models?'

'"Only You" by The Platters.'

'Excellent choice.'

'I think so.'

'And tell them, no cocaine.'

'Too late.'

'Well, then, we better get this done now. Thanks, Estelle.'

'And thank you, Miss Suze.'

'Very droll.'

'I try.'

'What would I do without you?'

'About sixty miles an hour over the Harbour Bridge.'

'Estelle!'

***

'Two Bloody Marys, you say?'

'Apart from the healthy celery, I have not eaten for three days. I am famished.'

'Not surprised. Are you still gobbling down methedrine? Caesar salad for me and a Pimms No. 2 Cup. Remember, I have got to wrap up before five this afternoon.'

'Diet pills darling, and, yes, they keep me trim and awake. The Duchess of Windsor said a girl cannot be too rich or too thin. Scampi, with mussels and artichoke, and a gin with prosecco and soda for me, please.'

'From vodka to gin. Must have been a big night!'

'You could say so. Took in a show at the Tivoli with school chums and kicked on at the Australia Hotel. Passed the time. So, tell me, what styles are in fashion for spring? Anything I would like?'

'There's a gorgeous pencil-slim one piece by Maggy Rouff. Such a smart designer. Pink and white dog's tooth check, offset with a flying panel at the rear. Sits on a low-set martingale belt. The clincher is a sublime hat by Erik. I am promoting it as the major picture from today's shoot. Maggy's one piece would suit you to a T. Do you realise gin is called "mother's ruin"?'

'Fat chance for me.'

'Don't say that, dear. You will find someone, Deborah. You must not give up.'

'That's the trouble. I don't want someone else. I want Ashton. Besides, most decent Aussie men are married and run big stations in the bush. I am not keen on becoming a jillaroo and wearing matching jodhpurs and Akubra from dawn to dusk. You are the only one of my friends who does not say "Get over it, it's in the past", and all that palaver. The fact is, I cannot forget him. And I still can't believe he died from a mosquito bite. If he went down with a gun in his hand in battle against the Japanese, I might feel different, but bloody malaria, for Christ's sake. I feel empty. I want to have children, and I wanted Ashton to be their father. I am not interested in other men and, God help me, I have had to fight one or two off with a feather duster.'

'You with a broom? Oh, my giddy aunt!'

'Ha! Well, you should hear what they say about you.'

'Who are they, and what do they say?'

'That you're Mata Hari's daughter.'

'For god's sake, she was Dutch. Let me tell you something scandalous about Margaretha Zelle – her real name – but I need to whisper in your ear.'

'Sounds exciting.'

'It seems she had two vaginas.'

'Oh god, I just swallowed my pink gin down the wrong way. Get me some water, please. I do not believe such a thing.'

'It's true, so they say, and apparently she had twice the fun before the firing squad finished her.'

'Oh, that's monstrous.'

'You have my permission to slip that titbit into the rumour stream, and what do you bet? It will come back around that I am the one with two vaginas, and a tail to boot.'

'You are so evil.'

'Who are these tell-tattles, anyway?'

'Tattletales, dear.'

'You shouldn't listen to gossip, Deborah.'

'Do you think such a thing exists?'

'I imagine so.'

'Could she conceive?'

'I am not sure. I am not a gynaecologist, but I doubt it, and if there was such a girl, I guarantee she would have been burnt at the stake as a witch like Joan of Arc.'

'Saint Joan?'

'The same. Joan wore men's clothes so soldiers would not rape her. You realise she spoke to angels and didn't menstruate?'

'Is that true? It's not normal, is it?'

'Who knows, but after she saved the country from the English, the French killed her. Typical. If you are in trouble, find a scapegoat, like in the Dreyfuss Affair.'

'What's that?'

'Never mind. Even better, blame a woman. Everyone knew Mata Hari flaunted her sexuality, but I feel certain she was not a spy, and there is no way she should have been shot.'

'Do you know communist spies operate in Australia?'

'I had no idea. Anyway, it is my turn to tell you something in strictest confidence, and if it comes back to me, I will know you tell-tattled.'

'Trust me, Suze.'

'I rarely menstruate.'

'Really?'

'My mother said several of our female relatives had a similar predisposition, but they lived normal lives and had families.'

'Is this why you haven't married?'

'I don't yearn to be a mother like you. I am not saying it will not happen, but there is no spark inside.'

'Anyone special in your life?'

'There is one fellow I adored, but romance didn't cross my mind.'

'What was he like?'

'Big, strong and fearless. Talked little and did what he was told.'

'The perfect man. And did you... you know?'

'My brother would have killed him if he looked sideways at me.'

'This is the first time I've heard you speak about your family.'

'Must be the Pimms.'

'I am terrified I will become an old maid like Miss Havisham. That book, *Great Expectations,* gave me the willies when we read it at Frensham. Dickens based Miss Havisham on a woman who's buried in St Stephen's Cemetery in Newtown.'

'Close to the New Theatre?'

'I am not sure where that is. Anyway, I can't remember her name, but we visited her grave on a school outing as part of our social studies of Caroline Chisholm. The difference between Miss Havisham and me is I didn't have a wedding dress to sit in all day. I framed your sketches of my wedding ensemble, by the way. They, and my butterfly brooch, are my most treasured possessions.'

'Thank you, dearest. How is old man Frost going?'

'Doddery. I think the place is going to the dogs. Last time I visited, he said I was in his will as Ashton's fiancé, but I doubt anything will come of it. He relies on Ossie for everything.'

'So, how does that work? An inheritance from a fiancé?'

'It's complex. My family is a big investor in the Frost Emporium. We grow cotton in Wee Waa. Anyway, the end products are sold in Frost stores. It was Ashton's idea. I was introduced to him when I turned sixteen, and our families agreed it was an ideal match.'

'An arranged marriage?'

'Sort of, but I fell in love with him and wanted to be married. Thinking back on it now, he was quite happy with his bachelor life.'

'And sex?'

'He didn't seem interested, but, if we'd married, I'd have made sure there would've been a house full of children.'

'I have got to get back to the studio. You are right about Ossie. He is a fine accountant. In fact, he urged me to buy shares in AWA. They are planning to make televisions for the mass market soon. Ossie reckons telephony is the future.'

'What does that mean?'

'Telephone technology. An acquaintance of mine in Austria tinkered with it ages ago. Her name is Eva Kiesler. She works in Hollywood now under the stage name Hedy Lamarr.'

'You are kidding me, Suze. You knew Hedy Lamarr?'

'Yes, but she was a serious girlie swat. Must run, Deborah.'

'Of course, dear, but there is one more thing I need to tell you.'

'What is it?'

'I'm hearing voices.'

'What sort of voices?'

'Screaming dead men.'

'Oh, Christ, Deborah!'

'I hear them at night.'

'What made you think about this?'

'I am a huge fan of the newsreels. I love the gossip about Her Majesty and Princess Margaret, but they slip in gruesome reports from Europe, Korea and Nagasaki.'

'The Korean War ended over ten years ago.'

'I know, but the Yanks wanted to use atomic bombs. I am terrified another war will break out to stop the communists in somewhere called Vietnam.'

'I don't watch newsreels, ever. Tell you what. Come and stay with me in Seaforth and help me buy a Halvorsen cruiser at Cottage Point.'

'I'd love to.'

'We'll drive over the Bridge in the Minx after I finish in the studio. Fresh sea air will do you a power of good.'

'I hope so.'
'And promise: no more diet pills.'
'I promise… well, for a week or so.'

12 Surabaya Jonny

I didn't know it at the time, but the trip to Cottage Point with Deborah led me to discover an unknown part of my being. It was where I met Aleta Berkenbosch, who sold stylish motor vessels to affluent customers at a select motor cruiser dealership. Aleta showed me a Sea Skiff measuring twenty-four feet bow to stern, ideal for a comfortable harbour crossing from Seaforth to Lady Jane Beach, where I could sketch landscapes to be finished as watercolours in my studio.

Aleta also taught sailing and seamanship. Under her tuition, I qualified for a maritime licence after mastering the fine art of motorboat cruising. Months later, I accepted her invitation to sail to Bali.

Aleta is older than me. She grew up on a rubber plantation in the prewar Dutch East Indies, now Indonesia. She married young and had three children with a Dutch military pilot who volunteered to fight in the Battle of Britain. Aleta never discussed his fate, and I assumed she never heard from him again.

She and her family fled the advancing Japanese aboard an evacuation flight on a Royal Netherlands Navy Air Service flying boat to Broome, Western Australia.

Aleta limps. Tracer fire from attacking Japanese Zeros grazed her hip and killed at least eighty-eight people, including her children, whom she buried in the Broome Pioneer Cemetery near the town's beach jetty.

I recall thinking about the details of her life on a humid day at the Darwin Sailing Club, surrounded by a band of tanned yachties lounging at the bar or playing cricket on a scorched patch of grass facing the bay. At first, I thought this assorted crew were locals, but most were vagabonds like us, from all points of the compass. Their vessels, like ours, bore the scars of an encounter with an east coast low pressure storm.

During that afternoon, we two female sailors of a battered but unscathed one-masted yacht named *Virgo* shared our story as part of a collective healing ritual.

Single men seemed uninterested in us, and we passed the day unhindered by drunken yobs with cheesy pickup lines. This type of behaviour didn't worry Aleta. She is bold and holds a man's gaze with unblinking eyes, whereas I am chatty and eager to relive our recent experience, to make sense of those hours and minutes when we prepared for the end.

Blue water sailing is the most challenging venture I have experienced. There were stretches of monotony interspersed with moments of panic, such as when a whale breached metres to starboard.

Before the storm hit us, a long cleft formed at the base of a bank of cumulonimbus. A golden glow transfigured its dark underbelly a pale aubergine. The spreading luminance caught the tip of cresting waves, and as a crevice in the mist widened, an unsettled patina gilded the sea with a coppery sheen. A spidery caulis of lightning cackled displeasure at the evaporating nimbus, and a crack of thunder warned we were a candidate for a strike, but the lustrous show made us courageous. A cascade of rain whispered into a half-curve rainbow, as a pod of dolphins surfed the face of the foaming gyre. We stayed alone on *Virgo's* deck, astounded as the darkness hemmed the ocean, which shone with bioluminescence.

For the umpteenth time, Aleta took me through procedures for abandoning ship: how to step into the life raft, which survival bag to grab, how to don a life jacket. Aleta estimated the rough weather at six on the Beaufort scale; on land, this meant large branches in motion and whistling in telegraph wires.

Roiling whitecaps rolled into the gloom. Cloaks of icy

rain cascaded from sodden cotton ball clouds. Brine-tainted horizontal showers misted our vision. As if a conductor urging *staccatissimo*, syncopated squalls, fast or intermittent, marked the rhythm of the plunging barometer. Nimble and resolute, Aleta let loose a small drogue from the stern before hoisting a storm sail to steady and trim *Virgo*.

A constant tattoo beat the sides of the hull as the angry eye coiled for miles off the far north Queensland coast. Like a naughty child in a bath, an invisible inverted hand pushed the waves to the brink of a turbulent sea before cresting above endless foamy sets. With a boom, a suck, and hiss, these whitecaps crashed against our hull.

Through the ages, storms of this size had shattered four-masted schooners, burying their crew up to their necks, their remains decayed to grains of sand buried beneath ancient cairns. Yet, somehow, we charted the Torres Strait and navigated across a calmer Arafura Sea before dropping anchor in Darwin.

This was my first big blow, and I knew there might be others as we navigated the Timor Sea to Kupang and the Savu Sea beyond. But that day at the decrepit Darwin Yacht Club, half listening to rumours about a violent anti-communist purge in Indonesia, I watched *Virgo* sway at its mooring in a murky bay and drank beer from longneck bottles as Aleta mapped out our next leg.

A life in the sun had darkened Aleta's skin, but her flesh was unblemished and smooth to the touch. She often stood naked on the deck. Once on a tranquil sea, she took up the sextant to calculate a dead reckoning of latitude and longitude, oblivious of a slight trickle of blood running the length of her inner thigh. Other times she wore a bikini brief and tee-shirt, whereas I wrapped myself in light scarves or Balinese batik and hid beneath wide-brimmed floppy hats.

I regarded Aleta as my love. On days of serenity and days of turmoil, I watched her traverse the deck, a lithe, strong ruler of her ship. And on those days, I whispered memorised cadenzas from the *Torah*:

> How fair and how pleasant art thou, O love, for delights! This thy stature is like to a palm tree, and thy breasts to clusters of grapes.

> Thy cheeks are comely with rows of jewels, thy neck with chains of gold. Many waters cannot quench love, neither can the floods drown it.

There is no more intimate setting than a couple navigating a yacht on the deep blue sea. Privacy doesn't exist. Life continues in full view of one another, which explains why yachties observe an unspoken rule. For the sake of onboard harmony, opinions should be kept neutral. Except for one time, Aleta and I followed this rule.

Let me explain.

We barely spoke in the days after the cyclone, but as she charted a course through the shallow Wessel Group, flanked by Graham and Drysdale islands, Aleta screamed at the radio.

'Fucking Jews,' she yelled.

Nothing more.

No explanation.

A burst of explosive anger.

Apart from a run-in with a testy Australian immigration officer about my expired passport, the rest of the voyage to Bali passed without incident.

I had gone through a single storm but succumbed to another.

As I think about those days at sea, I am unsure whether I am a better or worse person for abandoning Aleta in Surabaya. I am alone now and suspect so is she.

13 ZaSu presents

Months after I returned from Bali, Stanley Hull called, seeking my advice about a topic of which I knew nothing: television programming.

Stanley was employed by Sydney's major commercial television station, which broadcast daytime variety shows. Locating reliable talent proved a challenge. Stanley asked me to recommend luminaries from Sydney's fashionable set with the confidence to front the cameras and chat about everything from make-up to haute couture. These self-proclaimed experts had to be telegenic, eloquent and have enough chutzpah to attract sponsors to fund the time slot.

In the decade following the first television broadcast in Australia, Stanley worked on revues such as *Eunice Gardiner Presents,* which aired on Sundays at 5:30 pm. During the half-hour broadcast, the much-loved musician played piano and interviewed musical personalities between sets. Stanley introduced me to Eunice, and we became firm friends. I shared with her my fondness for classical music.

I recall asking Eunice where I could buy rare European recordings of symphonic pieces by Berg, Shostakovich, Mahler and Béla Bartók. She recommended Martin's on Pitt Street, which sold quality vinyl issued on the Melodiya and Deutsche Grammophon labels and pressed in the USSR. She warned I would be photographed if I ventured inside the record store. When I asked who took the photographs, thinking it must be newspaper people, her one word response stuck in my memory. ASIO. As for Shostakovich, Eunice had heard rumours members of the board of the New Theatre in Newtown planned to sponsor a tour of Australia by the maestro. According to

Eunice, ASIO watched the comings and goings of all the theatre's board members.

Stanley also produced four episodes of the variety show *Rendezvous at Romano's,* set in the swank Romano's restaurant and hosted by Harp Maguire. *Rendezvous* aired on Tuesday nights at 9:30 pm and featured Herbie Marks and his trio, and a woman known as "the lovely Miss Peggy Brooker".

He also managed *Town Talk,* presented by Robert Kennedy, the former presenter of *What's My Line. Town Talk* snared the coveted Friday evening slot of 7:15 pm, after the quarter hour news bulletin. But it was the twenty-seven minute *The World of Glamour* that caused Stanley the most bother, and he asked for my help. Each week, host Elaine White shone a spotlight on Sydney fashion and beauty. Sponsors competed to have their brands evaluated by the show's panel. These reviews became holy writ for scores of women who made up the bulk of the lucrative daytime and evening television market.

I convinced Ossie Jenkins to advertise the Frost wedding department on *The World of Glamour,* but the larger emporia maintained a bigger advertising spend and their constant spruiking of extensive ranges of women's products tended to drown out the Frost brand. I countered by suggesting Stanley take the show on the road to regional New South Wales to cover country weddings and important civil occasions. Stanley took my advice, and these rural promotions attracted lucrative agricultural sponsors, including winemakers from the Hunter Valley and growers of fine grade Merino fleece exported to Italy.

Stanley convinced me to appear as a design expert on *The World of Glamour,* despite my protestations that my accent would be a turn-off. Most on-air talent, he said, affected plummy Oxbridge inflexions or a cross between Canadian and American drawls, while authentic Australian voices remained unpopular with radio broadcasters or up-and-coming television presenters.

An Austrian burr, Stanley declared, might prove a hit with

an army of daytime mums, glued to fuzzy-pictured black-and-white TV sets, many tuned with the aid of coat hanger aerials.

Estelle suggested I give a presentation targeted at a younger audience. One program produced on her say-so caused an uproar, when a gum chewing model strutted across the sound stage wearing blue American jeans with rolled cuffs, bobby socks, off-white sneakers and an ivory tee-shirt with switched-back sleeves. A studded belt and an over-the-shoulder khaki jacket finished the ensemble. The switchboard of the TV channel was flooded with angry viewers, but I later heard that the stores which stocked the certain type of jeans sold out in a matter of days. A slew of advertisers spruiking clothes for teenagers then deluged the program, to the chagrin of Elaine White, who deemed her audience to be respectable daughters and dowagers, not pimply-faced debutantes.

Elaine's style choices sparked lively arguments in the green room, but while ever the advertising funds rolled in, management remained happy.

As a new though minor television personality, I gained entry to portions of Sydney I did not know existed. Each weeknight, fellow panellists, producers and crew moved from one nightclub to another. We spent evenings at Spellson's, followed by the Latin Quarter, or Attilio's. Bookings at Chequers proved difficult, whereas we were welcome at Romano's, the Silver Spade Room at the Chevron Hotel and Tabou. After the journalists let us be, we moved on to anonymous gambling dens to play fan-tan and baccarat, two-up and blackjack. The Goulburn Club, the roughest of these venues, was not to my taste, while a visit to the Mandarin Club often led to night crawls around Chinatown in search of an elusive opium den.

The next morning, it was back to the studio and a long session in make-up.

One of our stagehands knew a lighting man who worked on a Saturday morning racing program presented by Ken

Howard and "Clarence the Clocker". Their racing tips often resulted in sunny afternoons at Randwick racecourse for more betting, followed by evening parties made edgy by handfuls of Dexedrine, which kept everyone awake for a Sunday sunrise over Bondi Beach.

Gimmicks abounded. One presenter promoted their current American car, another a voyage to England on the newest P&O liner. I recollect a display of sleight-of-hand illusions. One person specialised in yodelling or off-colour ditties. I portrayed the character of a secretive woman who wore cat-eye sunglasses, or a partial veil connected to my newest fascinator, tailored for a formal ensemble. Everyone but me smoked on set. On one show, ash from a stubbed-out cigarette singed a portion of my lace glove. The ensuing on-air chaos ended up on the front pages of the afternoon papers, to the delight of station bigwigs, who hailed the so-called stunt worth a fortune in free advertising and revenue.

An enormous bouquet and a box of betting chips, valid at a certain Eastern Suburbs illegal casino, placated my fear of what could have been a disaster.

Despite the glitz, the perfume, the fur coats, none of our audience realised the ugly truth of the life of one panellist. A hairdresser to the stars and married to a person well-known amongst the racing fraternity, she described her dread of weekends. If her husband lost on the races, he would take it out on her, beating her back and shoulders with a White Pages phone book. She said he hit her this way because he 'did not want to bruise my pretty little TV face'.

Her religion made divorce unthinkable, plus she feared photographers who specialised in taking pictures of people caught in adulterous or lurid scenes. Ironically, she and her husband often appeared smiling and laughing in the social pages of the Sunday tabloids.

Over time, *The World of Glamour* fell out of favour, but

somehow my contract rolled on as a guest presenter of television specials recorded in large bush towns or attractive rural communities.

Ossie proposed I invest in securities and bonds from recently established local television channels, and, as always, the canny Mr Jenkins proved to be on the money.

14 Push

Estelle knocked on my office door and stepped in before I could respond.

'I want a raise.'

'Just like that?' I replied, trying to hide my shock. 'No please or thank you?'

'I have worked here for months. We both know you are struggling with orders, and without me, the whole thing fails. If you want me to stay, give me a raise.'

Her face and neck flushed deep scarlet as the mental calculations seemed to dance in her eyes: Have I gone too far? Will she sack me?

'We need to talk,' I replied. But now it was my turn to crank up the intellectual coruscations.

Though she worked part time, Estelle had become invaluable, and I could not continue without her. In German we say, *das Talent zu wissen, bevor man fragt*,[17] but her demeanour caught me short, and with this abruptness I thought she really might resign. Not ideal. I hoped her frankness would provide a face-saving compromise.

She opened up a little more. 'Mum is sick.'

'Why didn't you mention this earlier?'

'I'm telling you now, aren't I?' she said, eyes glistening and defiant.

'You live nearby?'

'With mum and my grandmother down near Riley Street.'

'Not too far from here.'

'That's right, but you don't want to go to Frog Hollow,' she replied, raising her hands, signalling the end of this strand of

[17] The talent of knowing before you ask

the conversation.

'And your father?'

'Killed during the war when I was a kid. He was a cobbler. Had a shop in the railway arcade in Central Station, but we own our terrace house.'

My mind raced in the ensuing silence. I am hopeless at management and staff matters. I am Estelle's boss, but I must come across as a greedy employer not paying a fair wage for a fair day's work. On her days with me, she opens the terrace before I arrive, leaves on my say-so, sometimes seven or eight o'clock at night, and works weekends unless I tell her not to come. She runs my office, checks couriers in and out, keeps my diary, answers and screens phone calls, collaborates with photographers setting up dozens of shoots a week, and yet I had not offered her an increase, let alone a Christmas bonus. My turn to blush with guilt.

'I watch everything you do with your designs,' she said. 'I have learnt so much. Mum says I should ask you to take me on as an apprentice. She and Gran do piecework in the rag trade, but mum's crook with a lung infection from dust, we think. I want to learn how you do it.'

'Do what?'

'Design hats, dresses, bits and pieces.'

'It's second nature,' I replied, sensing a thaw in the mood. 'I have done this for as long as I can remember.'

'Yes, but how?'

'I will tell you, but for now just be content with a raise. I will talk with Mr Jenkins and figure out a decent rate, plus backpay to help out, and I promise you an annual performance review.'

What happened next left me breathless. Estelle kissed me on the mouth, and I did not pull away.

'Thank you so much. I am taking us out to celebrate.'

I broke from her embrace and nodded, lost for words.

'Where are we going?'

'We'll have a girls' New Year's Eve get-together. We can walk or grab a cab. My shout.'

But when you need a taxi, they are never around, so we ambled downhill to Darling Harbour, where I had come ashore in Australia.

Office workers and wharf labourers mingled in the top bar. A sign pointing to the bistro reminded me I had not eaten since breakfast. Laughter and singing spilled out from an area at the rear of the hotel called the Ladies Lounge.

Estelle took my hand and tugged me into the midst of a gaggle of laughing, dancing women, some sitting at the bar, others waiting to be served. At least five staff stood behind the counter, pulling beers, taking money and chatting with regulars.

Estelle greeted people as she weaved to a table near a jukebox. I could barely hear the names of the women she introduced, but when we settled down with gins and tonic she said 'Cheers' and thanked me for the raise. 'You don't have a clue how much this means.'

I sipped my drink and asked her about the pub.

'The bar caters for women who enjoy the company of other women, such as you and me.'

'How do you mean?'

'Oh, come on, Suze, don't play the innocent with me!' she exclaimed, upending her G&T. 'I'll get us another.'

I declined. 'I'm fine for now. I need to eat; otherwise, this gin will knock me for a six.'

'Sounds like a plan, then I'm taking us out for a surprise.'

As Estelle disappeared, a group of women huddled at the jukebox, dropped coins in a slot, and began singing in unison at the top of their voices.

The room erupted with cheering, and with the last refrain, couples peeled off to slow dance.

'This is a lot of fun,' I said when Estelle returned to the table, now shared with two other women.

'They're a good crew. This is a Push pub. Lucky for us, the licensee is tolerant. She makes a motza every night of the week.'

I was glad to be free of the smoke-filled lounge, but as I was about to enter the bistro, Estelle called my name. As I turned, an unknown girl planted a kiss on my cheek. A flashbulb popped, blinding me for a moment. Another bulb lit up the room as the stranger ran her fingers through my hair. I pulled free and walked into the dining room.

'Who was that?' I demanded, blinking to regain my focus. 'And where did you get that camera?'

'Steady on. It's a celebration. I want to remember this as the night my life changed for the better. I borrowed it from a photographer. He's teaching me about f-stops and aperture settings and lenses. Too much for me to follow.'

My head swam from the gin. Tonic sweetened Estelle's breath. My stomach growled from hunger. At last, we tucked into heaped portions of pub fare. I relaxed and let the ambience wash over me.

'So, tell me more about the Push,' I said.

'To be honest, I haven't got a clue, but I think it means it's time for change in Australia. People get together and drink and argue about where this country is heading, or what it should be like in the future.

'Pubs around the city, especially over in Glebe and Forest Lodge near Sydney University, have their own push where they debate politics. The mob up in the Cross print pornographic newspapers and dare the Vice Squad to close them down. Here, women feel safe. They can be themselves except for the occasional raid.

'There's a big jar in the manager's office stuffed with cash. Whenever a Crown sergeant comes in, whoever is on duty "contributes" to the Police Boys Club. Everyone chips in when the jar is empty. It's a tax of sorts, but we're prepared to contribute just to be left alone.

'There are women here tonight who are "on the game" and others who work on the docks with the men. The Vice Squad gets iffy over prostitution or cross-dressing, which is a crime, I think. So, the jar stays full. Cops from the Pillage Squad drink here, but they don't give a fuck. They've seen it all. This, Suze, is the Royal George Hotel.'

'And where is this soiree?'

'Chatswood.'

With only one G&T, I figured I could drive, and afterward cut across country to Seaforth.

'Who are the hosts?'

'Not sure. People of your age and…'

'And what?'

'They've got LSD.'

'Never heard of it,' I replied. 'How does it work?'

'Crazy hallucinations. What the hell, it's New Year's Eve. Next year, more Telstars will rocket into space, and orbit above us,' she said, pointing to the ceiling. 'Welcome to the future, Suze. Let's be a part of it. Shall we go?'

I nodded but said I would drive.

'Risky, but fine with me,' she replied.

We walked back to the office, picked up my car and drove into a traffic jam on the Harbour Bridge.

Estelle found the house, a single-storey double-brick bungalow, set back on a deep block in a leafy, suburban locale. The front door was latched, but open, the interior tastefully mid-century modern. Yma Sumac sang "Gopher Mambo" as a half dozen bare-footed guests, absorbed in their dance, gestured in the air, oblivious of those around them. Marijuana smoke filled the crowded lounge room. The pub had been raucous and friendly, but these guests appeared subdued. A girl with long hair and a part down the middle of her skull sobbed quietly in a corner, comforted by an attentive companion.

'It's the LSD,' Estelle said. 'Do you want a tab?'

'What do I do?'

'Give me your forefinger,' she said, placing a tiny dot on the tip of my finger, which promptly slipped into my fingernail.

'Don't worry, just suck your finger.'

I did as I was told.

'You'll feel it in about twenty minutes,' Estelle said, drifting away. 'See you on the other side.'

A casually dressed man sat down next to me. 'And what line of work keeps you busy?'

'Fashion design. And you?'

'I'm researching electron paramagnetic resonance,' he said, but as I asked him to explain, a young woman whispered in his ear.

'Gotta go,' he said. 'Happy New Year.'

'And you,' I replied.

The music changed to Miles Davis's "Kind of Blue". I closed my eyes, and for an hour, drifted in and out of the most sublime tonal shifts.

The flash of a camera bulb broke my reverie. When the glare subsided, I looked for Estelle, but could not find her in the kitchen, the lounge or other rooms occupied by people in various stages of undress.

A male voice said, 'Happy New Year, friends, and fellow travellers. Here's to a better year.'

After a chorus of 'Hip hip hooray', I scanned the house once more but could not locate Estelle.

Time to go. I drove at the speed limit to Roseville Bridge, through Forestville, and turned right into the Wakehurst Parkway. A red-blue light blinked in my rear-view mirror. I pulled over. The policeman asked if I had had anything to drink.

'A gin and tonic about six o'clock yesterday,' I said.

He ordered me out of the car, examined my licence, and told me to close my eyes and stand on one foot.

I complied.

'Can I open my eyes now?'

'What is your accent?'

'Austrian.'

'I don't want you going into the Austrian Club,' he said, pointing at a building nestled in nearby bushland. 'Where do you live?'

'Seaforth,' I replied. 'It's on my licence.'

'On your way. If I see you again, I'll book you.'

'For what?'

'I'm sure I'll find a bald tyre,' he said. 'Now go.'

I got home, put the key in my front door, poured a wine, and settled down to watch the New Year twinkle over the city skyline.

I noticed a blotch under my fingernail. The LSD tab.

'I'm too tired,' I said aloud, and walked to my bedroom, found a tissue, wrapped up the little dot and placed it in the medicine cabinet.

Next morning, I drove to the supermarket, stocked up on groceries, bought the papers and decided on an afternoon sail on the harbour aboard my cruiser, but a front-page headline scuppered my plans: Two bodies found in Lane Cove National Park.

The ABC midday news bulletin identified the male as Dr Gilbert Bogle and the female as Margaret Chandler. The evening news reported both had attended a New Year's Eve get-together in Chatswood and described Dr Bogle as 'an eminent scientist specialising in paramagnetic resonance', and Mrs Chandler as 'a Sydney housewife'.

Day after day the tabloids published lurid headlines featuring speculative stories about the cause of their deaths, and, although I had only briefly met Dr Bogle, Estelle's erratic behaviour, and the random photographs, triggered a spate of paranoid night terrors.

15 Spy craft

Several of Noel O'Grady's trusted comrades knew a great deal about Nicholas Treloar. I never discovered how or why they came by this information, but they were more than happy to pass on anecdotes. I often wondered if a union member fed information about Treloar back up the line. My supposition seemed improbable, but during the Cold War era in Australia, Nicholas Treloar's lifelong interest in me was just as unlikely.

His colleagues called him the Top Boy, or Top for short. Over decades as a senior intelligence officer, he earned a slew of sobriquets, including the Black Prince for successful work on the Verona intercepts at the Agincourt building in Potts Point. But his favourite nickname remained the Red Terror, bestowed for his adroit management of the handler of Dr Michael Bialoguski during the so-called Petrov Affair in 1954.

Nicholas pressed an intercom button.

'Eileen, grab your shorthand pad, please.'

Eileen Coyle, a friend of Eunice Gardiner, and who also served on the board of the New Theatre, had worked with Nicholas Treloar from the early days in Potts Point. Eileen knew the system backward.

'Dig out the Noel O'Grady file.'

'Australian Workers Union?' Eileen asked.

'A memory like a steel trap, Miss Coyle.'

'And what do you need?'

'Open a new file cross-referencing all the O'Grady matters.'

'Under what name, Top?'

'Susan Lieder.'

'The morning TV hostess?'

'That's the one.'

'Does she have an alias?'

'ZaSu,' Nicholas said, 'and while you are at it, I want an update on Estelle Riley's reports. Might as well get a full picture of what O'Grady and Miss ZaSu have been up to.'

Nicholas Treloar had opposed his organisation's recent name change from the Commonwealth Investigation Service and the transfer to a permanent office building in Canberra, a city, he said, designed by a nonconformist American to serve citizens incapable of safely navigating roundabouts.

He listened politely as upper management extolled the virtues of their country lives in the Southern Highlands of New South Wales or the dappled delights of the Dandenong Ranges outside Melbourne. But, when his turn came, Nicholas said those who threatened the safety of the nation live in hovels and rats' nests in Fitzroy, Rozelle, Redfern and Camp Hill, where, he insisted, 'our efforts must be concentrated'.

He decided to read *The Manifesto of the Communist Party* in the weeks after the Battle of Stalingrad and became convinced a Red Army of Australian unionists would smooth the way for cadres of Soviet comrades. Passing around the hat at rallies for the New Theatre or chook raffles at the Trades Hall could barely finance the price of a new FJ Holden let alone the cost of publishing *Tribune* or the *Queensland Guardian,* and its equivalent in Melbourne, plus a myriad other communist ventures.

How these local communists funded their domestic activities remained a mystery, and he had briefed one of his best field officers, Estelle Riley, to spy on me. I first met Nicholas Treloar on the day I disembarked ship at Darling Harbour.

The Top Boy wrote memos in triplicate, theorising that a stream of gold poured out of the USSR and into union coffers, but after decades of service keeping the nation safe, he failed to uncover its source. He argued with anyone prepared to listen that the trade in Soviet bullion coincided with the influx of enemy aliens at the outbreak of war, but now, this narrow band of suspects withered with the post-war immigration boom.

'And tell Graeme we have a briefing in ten minutes.'

Graeme Hanna boasted four rugby caps, two cauliflower ears and a broken nose after playing as an open side flanker in the number seven jersey. Strong and fit, Hanna weighed somewhere between 240 and 250 pounds. This lighter frame enabled him to get to breakdown areas quickly and disrupt opposition play; ideal on-field attributes, or useful in a brawl with wharfies, dockside. After his final year as dux at the Kings School, and between rugby engagements, Hanna graduated with second-class honours in economics at Oxford. A first-rate field officer, he preferred the outdoors to desk work.

'Fancy a trip to Western Australia?'

'Not Basil again?' Graeme rolled his eyes.

'I'm afraid so, me old cock.'

'Debited from the standard leger?' Eileen Coyle asked.

'No. This one is billed to Whitehall.'

'In that case, the Exchequer needs a file name. Do I go with the usual, Castle Howard?'

'Yes.'

'We'll need to specify a sum of British pounds.'

'Leave it blank please and draw up the documentation for the Director-General's signature. I'll have him verify the amount once he's briefed Graeme and myself.'

'Will do, and I presume standard travel allowance, accommodation vouchers for two, plus an unmarked Z car at every stop?'

'And double rations of quinine tablets,' Graeme interjected.

A ratcheting up of insurgency in Malaya, nasty rumblings from Indonesia, plus the Dutch meekly allowing Western New Guinea to slip into Indonesia's grasp, distracted the Top's desk from investigating the ongoing domestic threat of the Red Menace.

When his Director-General mentioned yet another consultation with MI6 operative Basil Howard in Wyndham in Western Australia, Nicholas knew he would lose precious months in his search for the source of Soviet gold. Thus, a fresh update on O'Grady and me might turn something up.

In the meantime, he had to brief a man he loathed. Treloar considered Basil Howard the opposite of the idealised image of an urbane MI6 operative. When his Director-General used the word 'liaise', Nicholas knew a wet job beckoned in a tropical outpost of the ever-shrinking British Empire; the loathsome Howard would once again become the man of the moment.

The Top Boy abhorred the garrotte, believing it a cowardly weapon, used by gangsters and dagos. Basil used a short length of easily disposable fishing line. Once the "fish" had been "snagged", Basil Howard returned to obscurity in a humpy outside Wyndham and hung another grisly flip-flop sandal trophy on a heavily laden thong tree. Then, with an endless supply of gin, shipped into the port aboard flat-bottomed coastal cattle scows, Howard resumed his mission of drinking himself to death in the company of an Aboriginal girl.

'How long do you expect to be away?' Eileen asked, sensing the briefing about to end.

'I'll take this up with the Director-General, but to be on the safe side, book international travel chits with Qantas.'

One night over a few wines at the New Theatre, a tipsy Eileen told me she walked to the door and strained to overhear details of Basil's mission.

Nicholas had swivelled in his chair, placed a finger to his lips and said to Graeme, 'Probably some tinpot commissar.'

'After we sober him up,' Graeme replied.

Nicholas chuckled.

'He's at his most dangerous once he gets to the other side of the delirium tremens,' he said. 'Grumpy as all get-out. Thank you, Eileen.' Graeme mouthed a question. 'Eavesdropping?'

'Wouldn't expect anything less,' Nicholas said. 'A word to the wise, Graeme. Never lie, hide everything in full view, and do not trust anyone.'

'Including you, Top?'

'Without a doubt me, old cock.'

Not one operative in the organisation – Graeme Hanna, Eileen Coyle, the knighted Director-General, the Canberra spooks or any undercover agents – trusted the Top Boy, a scenario encouraged by Nicholas Treloar.

16 *Teyerste meydl mit das zisste harts*[18]

I collect stamps. Most are of little value, but I love the image of Her Majesty posed in an array of colours, from diverse parts of the Empire, or stamps from the wider world. The watermarks suggest certainty, the different shapes and hues, and the range of currencies (ringgit, rupee, US dollar, British pound) are in denominations equal, I guess, to threepence or sixpence. Then there are the wafer thin, glued aerograms, with spidery text filling every inch of space. And letters in flimsy envelopes marked Par Avion. I have boxes of them, mostly business correspondence from the United States Navy, and mail from friends, secured by a rubber band. But I have none from my family in Austria or England.

I had never seen correspondence such as this – a letter inside a letter. The outer envelope addressed to me, but to the wrong address in Seaforth, then redirected to the Frost head office and finally my studio in Commonwealth Street. Each variation marked with an official GPO stamp and adorned with anonymous initials scrawled inside an inked stamped box. At the top left-hand corner, the imprint of CofA (Commonwealth of Australia) inside a circle, and on the back, a return address to Canberra in the Australian Capital Territory, adorned with yet another stamp of a finger pointing to a name, Miss Sally B. Luxford, and an address.

I boiled the kettle and willed the steam to melt the glue. Finally, I lifted the intact paper flap. Inside, another letter. The outside of the second envelope, covered in notations read, 'Opened by the Australian Censor on authority of the Department of Defence'. Again, on the top left-hand side,

---

[18] Dearest girl with the sweetest heart

the letters CofA surrounded by a circle, but adorned with an adjacent squat, arrow-like symbol. I made out the imprint of the value of a halfpenny. The envelope had been slit open, marked by the Censor, and resealed with a strip of tape. As I opened the older letter, the dry glue disintegrated into crumbs and settled at its bottom. When I read the word "Hay", I knew it was Leo.

An age passed before I could read the text. He had torn paper from a child's lined school textbook. Creases obscured portions of the lettering, but the writing proved the biggest surprise, an admixture of Hebrew and Yiddish. A question mark sliced through my name, and a circle enclosed another name, plus faded notes in the margins. One note read, 'What does this mean? We need a translator.' 'What is the language?' another demanded.

And I read:

> Apologies, Shoshanna. My Hebrew is worse than my Yiddish, but I hope the script slows down their attempt to translate. You can be sure the authorities open this because of my status.
>
> Time is short.
>
> Your family's treasure is safe. With your permission, I would like to invest in land and stock here in Hay. If I manage to do this, I will register the property in our names.
>
> Your mother Ruth packed jewellery in the trunk's lining; a hatpin, necklaces, and rings.
>
> It is all stored in a strongbox under my name in the Hay branch of the Commonwealth Bank, where I am detained with other Europeans. The bank manager holds a letter of authority naming you, but a Mr Noel O'Grady of The Australian Workers Union has the key. Find his address. Show this letter to him with proof of

your identity. Noel travels the country organising union membership, so he might be hard to track down.

All I can say is I love you with all my heart. Seeing you again and daydreaming about life on the land is all I have. The rest belongs to you.

Ale meyn libe,[19]
Leo

I stopped breathing when I read my mother's name. My hands trembled. Estelle barged in after I had blown my nose repeatedly, demanding to know what was wrong. All I could say was, 'Tea.'

Estelle flounced back to the kitchen, rattled cups, and made a show of banging the kettle and filling it with water.

I ached for my mother, my father, Rudolph, and Leo. I read and re-read his words… *I love you with all my heart.* As I drew breath, I felt joy, but with the next intake, the throb of loss punched my chest.

'Do you want me to stay over tonight?'

'Do you mind?'

'Of course not. You will do your Greta Garbo routine. *I vant to be alone.*'

'You make me laugh. Thanks.'

'Have a sip of my special brandy infused brew.'

'That's strong. Just what I need.'

'Sounds to me like it's time for another overseas holiday.'

'I wish, but I've got serious problems with travelling.'

'Why?'

'I let my passport expire.'

'Easy enough to get a replacement.'

'Not for me. It's complicated.'

'If you get a new one, where would you go?'

'England first, to try to find my mother and father, then Europe, and finally Austria, to sort out family matters.'

---

[19] All my love

'I'd love to go to England.'

'London is special.'

'What's Austria like?'

'Now you have made me cry again. I am just a blubbering idiot.'

'This hit you hard.'

'Do you know the song "Love Hurts", sung by Roy Orbison?'

'Sure do. Fantastic singer.'

'There's a line in this letter which says *Teyerste meydl mit das zisste harts,* and this is what is making me cry.'

'What does it mean?'

'Dearest girl with the sweetest heart,' I said, and sobbed.

17 Solidarity

I had rehearsed this meeting at least a hundred times, mulling over what I might, and what I should and should not, say.

I knocked and waited.

A secretary answered. 'Can I help you?'

'I'm here to meet Mr O'Grady.'

'Hang on, dear.'

The secretary ducked out of sight, but I could hear the conversation within.

'There's a lady outside.'

'Who is she?'

'I don't know, but she needs to see you.'

'I need more bloody information than that.'

'Watch your language, Noel, for Christ's sake. She asked about a bloke called Leo Hulbert.'

'Well, I'll be dipped in sheep shit.'

'What's your name, dear?'

'Susan Lieder.'

'Her name is—'

'Yeah, I heard. Any chance of a cuppa? Come in, please, Miss Lieder. Move those files off the chair and make yourself comfortable.'

'Mr Noel O'Grady?' I asked.

'Call me Noel. None of this "mister" bullshit. What can I do you for? I am the Assistant General Secretary of the Australian Workers Union, and I gather you are a friend of Leo? I haven't heard his name in yonks.'

'How do you have your tea, dear?'

'Black with two sugars.'

'Here you go, love.'

'Where's my tea?'

'Get your own, Noel.'

'Hang on. Must have a cuppa. Do you mind if we shut the door?'

'Go right ahead,' I answered.

'Bear with me, I've got member files up the wazoo,' Noel said, as he rummaged through documents crammed inside a rickety wooden filing cabinet.

'Ah ha,' Noel said triumphantly. 'Leo Hulbert.'

'He had a file?'

'Yep. He is a union member, but unfinancial by now. Here's the date I signed him up, when he paid his fees, plus copies of union brochures circulated to the membership. And there are these.' Noel handed me a letter with my name written on the front and another marked "ZaSu" and stamped with a Bulgarian postmark. 'I'd be right in saying that these are why you came to see me?'

'Yes.'

'So, how did you track me down?'

'A long story,' I said. 'Leo suggested I prove my identity.' I placed the documents on his desk. 'Here is my driver's licence, my out-of-date passport, and Leo's letter. I assure you all are genuine.'

Noel adjusted his spectacles.

'A good bloke,' he said, handing me the letters, which I placed inside my handbag.

'What's the full story? You're from Sydney, and you know Leo was in the pokey in Hay, and, for the record, how did you find me in Melbourne?'

I sipped my tea.

'From a man I met in Canberra,' I replied. 'He ordered me to watch you whenever you visit Sydney and report back to him; otherwise, he'll prosecute me for entering Australia on forged papers.'

The blood drained from Noel's face.

'Are you fair dinkum?' he demanded.

I nodded.

Noel swore at the top of his voice, but he eventually calmed down and asked me to repeat the story to curious colleagues who had barged into his office to discover the cause of the commotion.

I stammered as I retold my tale, finishing with, 'I said I would watch him, but I did not tell him that I would check with Mr O'Grady first, and this is why I am here.' I spilt tea into the saucer.

'They know everything about this union's politics, so what the fuck is going on?' a youthful official demanded.

More unionists crammed into the smoky room.

'This whole thing must have something to do with a strongbox Leo left in the Commonwealth Bank which belongs to this lady.' Noel turned back to me. 'Any idea what's inside?'

'My family's property,' I replied.

I outlined my relationship with Leo, our journey to Australia, and how he ended up with a travelling trunk containing my family's possessions.

Noel listened in silence. When I finished speaking, he described how he and Leo had become acquaintances in the internment camp, how Leo joined the union, the chronic labour shortage, Leo's willingness to work wherever he could help, and his volunteering to join the AIF. He described Leo's last day in Hay and the encounter with police. With Noel's detailed story, the circle of decades of our separation closed.

'So, what did this nark in Canberra say to you?'

'He demanded I tell him about my dealings with a scientist and a woman found dead on a riverside track in Lane Cove,' I said. 'He accused me of taking drugs and joining in orgies. He showed photographs of women embracing me. I don't have a clue who they are, but he called me a perverted lesbian and accused me of deceiving Australian authorities. And he said I collaborated with this union to destabilise the country by allowing communists to infiltrate the body politic. The truth is I know nothing about these allegations.'

A hot-headed union official broke the silence. 'So, why risk your neck to tell Noel?'

I picked up my cup, drained the tea, and drew a deep breath. 'Because I've seen it happen before. Government officials turn people against each other with threats, intimidation and extortion. Then gangs of thugs roam the streets, saluting flags hung on every corner, and bash people who refuse to obey. They threaten to inform on your friends and family if you refuse to comply.

'Eventually, everyone becomes a telltale. The same nonsense appears in the newspapers and on the radio, in the cinemas and on the newsreels, and without realising you begin to adjust your day-to-day life to cope with constant, low-level fear.

'I decided decades ago I would not live this way. I have not nor will ever bow to them, and I will never be an informer.'

'Do you know who dobbed you in to this prick?' Noel asked.

I replied with a simple nod.

'Fucking dog,' Noel said to the accompaniment of a chorus of hissing and swearing.

'And this is what he gave me to write up my reports about your movements,' I said, handing Noel a notepad, with a gold Commonwealth of Australia emblem stamped on the cardboard cover.

'You know you might be deported,' Noel said.

'If it comes to that, then so be it.'

'I don't think we can let that happen,' Noel said.

'What do you mean?'

'If this arsehole wants to snoop on me – or members of this union – then we'll give him a show he won't forget. Time we let them know the jig's up. Fuck 'em.'

A chorus of 'fair enough' rippled around the room.

'The Hay races are coming up shortly,' said Noel. 'So, we'll put on a shearing competition, and Miss Lieder here can stump up the purse.'

'The district newspapers will cover it, and with a bit of luck, so will the local television station,' Noel said.

The secretary chimed in. 'You wouldn't mind posing for a picture with Noel, would you, dear?'

'Nah, she wouldn't mind, and she can hand over a dummy strongbox with the prize money inside,' Noel said.

Peals of laughter changed the mood from anger to defiant celebration.

With Noel's permission, I jotted inflated details of our meeting in my special pad.

True to his word, Noel circulated information about the competition to the nation's shearers and following some not-so-gentle persuasion, Hay councillors agreed to set aside the local showground for the big competition.

When I returned to Sydney, I made sure Estelle had access to my notebook, filled with details about my meeting with Noel O'Grady and other union officials.

If Estelle was as competent a spy as I imagined, the citizens of Hay would not only host gangs of shearers, and a big turnout of media, they would unknowingly have a muster of spies in their midst.

18 Bachelors and spinsters

I recall the weeks and months of long-distance planning for the shearing competition as a highlight of my life.

A member of the planning committee asked me to formally receive the debutantes at the Bachelors and Spinsters Ball, set down for the final night of the races. I accepted, but, with the time needed to prepare, I decided to stay over in Hay for a few weeks.

I am like most people who pass through the countryside as passive observers, not as participants in its life and moods. A rural existence has never been integral to my being, but during my time in Hay, in tiny ways, I experienced events I imagined Leo would have loved. I understood why he dreamt of settling on the Murrumbidgee plains, and I take heart in the knowledge he included me and my kin in his plan. When I think about it, mine was the only family Leo ever knew.

A local convent run by the Presentation Sisters provided my accommodation. I knew little of the sisters' work but learnt their order helps the needy by educating inexperienced women from around the world.

The Hay monastery, named Waroowarung, and built by a well-known local family, comprises a dozen rooms adorned with marble mantelpieces. The interior is connected by a wide hall and spacious passages. The cloister's roof is made of French tiles imported from Marseilles. Stained cathedral windows decorate the ornamental front door.

Waroowarung is a short walk from the Sandy Point Beach Reserve on the banks of the Murrumbidgee. I spent pleasant evenings on this beach, warming my hands around a fire in the company of visitors camped by the river. As I stared into the embers, I pondered my life and future and reflected on the sisters' commitment to encouraging young women to be the best they can be.

My mother Ruth admired the silent Carmelite nuns, secluded in the Carmelite monestry in Döbling, Vienna, built at the close of the 19th century. She told me about the origin of their order. Jewish and Christian hermits lived, prayed and taught in caves on Mount Carmel, a locale sacred to the prophets Elijah and Elisha.

And, like my mother, I am awestruck by women who take a vow to dedicate their life to silent contemplation. I too am part of a community of women. Through art, we dedicate each brushstroke and every curved and nuanced line as an offering to the good of all. I meditated upon on these things as riverine animals prepared for night, and the evening star rose above the Old Man Plain.

I visited the sites of the internment camps and donated to a newly formed museum which holds exhibits of photographs, memorabilia and stories describing the experiences of the thousands of German, Italian and Japanese civilian internees and prisoners of war, who were housed in the three camps, from 1940 to 1946.

News of my friendship with Leo filled the town's bush telegraph. People stopped me on the street, eager to reminisce.

The Commonwealth Bank manager escorted me to a nook next to the bank vault and told me to take my time examining the contents of the strongbox. I collected my mother's jewellery and counted the gold coins. I felt detached and unemotional.

Alone with my thoughts inside that airless room, I decided to buy land in the district, for Leo, my family and myself.

A real estate agent with an Italian surname mentioned that his father had been an internee. After inspecting several properties, I chose a large block with permanent water and a sturdy colonial era house.

Though his hands are gnarled with arthritis, Noel officiated the shearing competition, which attracted competitors from Queensland, South Australia and New Zealand. The winner, a gigantic Kiwi, lifted me above his head as I clutched the phoney strongbox with the prize money, and roared defiance at the local shearers. Cameras popped and TV crews jostled for close-ups, ideal for the evening news.

Meanwhile at the races, an official called over the public address system, appealing 'To the bastard who towed away the starting gates, bring the bloody thing back!'

The owner of a semitrailer that was parked near the oval sold bottles of chilled champagne. People wandered the paddocks, swigging from the bottles, chatting, laughing, and arguing the merits of horses readying for the upcoming race.

As I sat in a group, a man handed me a balloon, which he gripped by the neck. He instructed me to open it ever so lightly next to my mouth, inhale, close, and pass to the next person. The nitrous oxide gas lifted my head off my shoulders.

I recall the man saying, 'Laughing gas is a hundred times better than any dentist in Hay.' My jaw ached from laughter, and I joined him upending a bottle of champagne.

My memories of the remainder of the evening are hazy, except for one of the most exquisite spectacles I had ever seen. Young men wearing uniforms of Cuban heeled boots, tight denim jeans, leather belts with large buckles, check shirts with raised collars and broad-brimmed hats entered the arena and walked to the stage. As if a flock of birds perched on a wire, dark-skinned ringers sat on the top bar of a steel fence encircling the packed showground. Onlookers whistled and cheered or performed burnouts in their utes on the oval. But the raucous din fell to pin drop silence as a confluence of timid debutantes approached the stage, lit by a pale, waning yellow moon rising over the flat horizon. Perfume scented the still night air. The click of stiletto heels on the timber floor; the singular sound as they approached me. I shook their hands and watched as they each collected a bouquet of wildflowers. Then, facing their partner, each girl reached out a hand, and, to the opening bars of Bingham's cotillion, began a perfectly squared dance, in the style of a quadrille.

A Presentation Sister took my arm, leant to my ear and whispered, 'We spent hours on rehearsals, but I can tell you, this is the best day of my life. I am proud beyond words.'

19 Gerontius

During my stay in Hay, browsing museum exhibits and retracing Leo's steps, I realised my life was passing by. I thought about those I cherished, those I had lost, my family and Leo, and the people who kept me centred during my time in Australia. Even though contact with Deborah was always brief, the memories of my short television career helped me stay in touch with her brother Stanley. But, to my surprise, the person who served as my anchor during the tumult of the war and the following decades was a mild-mannered accredited accountant who directed the affairs of one of Sydney's finest emporiums.

Only a few Frost staff knew him as Oswald. Punctual, quietly spoken and expert with numbers, he was Jenkins or Ossie to everyone else, particularly Jeremiah Frost, who, as I discovered, increasingly relied on his advice.

I suspect Ossie confided in me in part because of an older man's mild infatuation, but probably more because I repaid his unstinting financial advice by introducing him to a world alien to the cohort of accountants with whom he associated.

Ossie told me his wife Davina, who loathed the habit of truncating names, insisted on calling him Oswald Jenkins. Davina suspected Ossie of jettisoning the formality of the post-war years, a mode of behaviour she endorsed. One morning before leaving their Turramurra home for work, Ossie watched Davina rummage through his cherished Gladstone bag, a present from his grandfather and decorated with a solid silver clasp. He had left the ancient satchel in a corner of his home office and swapped it for a smooth, crocodile skin briefcase. Ossie avoided a clash with his wife because inside his new valise sat a contract for a top-of-the-line Rambler Ambassador motor car. He told me with pride that he chose this model because of its longer wheelbase. A car dealer on upper William Street in East Sydney promised a tidy trade-in on Ossie's reliable Humber Super Snipe Series II.

American technology and manufacturing techniques enthralled Ossie, who bought shares in up-and-coming Australian companies transitioning to sunrise industries. His expanding portfolio of stock in aviation, telephony, and impending colour television, rose steadily in value. He monitored the progress of Australasian Wireless Limited, or AWA, and its joint venture with the Radio Corporation of America, producing defence electronics materiel at a plant in Ashfield. Though hush-hush, he learnt about klystron valves and magnetrons for radar, via his contacts in the War Ministry.

An avid reader of and subscriber to *Popular Mechanics* magazine, Ossie realised the demand for colour television sets would equal or surpass the craze for Formica furniture, Pyrex cookware, asbestos construction sheeting and twin-tub washing machines. If Frost wanted to stay ahead of upstart retailers such as H. G. Palmer with its unregulated credit schemes, the proprietary limited company needed robust distribution contracts with local manufacturers to promote and sell the most expensive consumer device ever launched in Australia. Ossie believed Jeremiah didn't comprehend television's potential or the increasing demand for plastic radios, which grew smaller due to the conversion from valve technology to transistors. Ossie browsed newsagents for magazines with articles about impressive gadgets such as EDSAC, the Electronic Delay Storage Automatic Calculator, developed by researchers at Cambridge University. As transistor technology became more manageable, he knew the same would happen with calculators.

He asked about the camouflage designs I undertook during the closing years of the war, and, although I had signed the *Official Secrets Act* and told him I could not speak about my work in detail, I showed him how a sequence of well-thought-out patterns, painted in the colours of a landscape, could make an object disappear.

As the only female civilian member of the Sydney Camouflage Group of artists, photographers, architects and other specialists, I conducted research at the Defence Central Camouflage Committee based at Georges Heights. The committee took its orders from the Australian Army general command, which demanded civilians such as me who designed camouflage patterns remain silent about our duties, under threat of prosecution.

My work as a camoufleur allowed me to introduce Ossie to contemporary art, particularly the work of female Australian artists of whom he had no knowledge. I explained the importance of Judy Cassab, Margaret Olley, Grace Cossington Smith, Thea Proctor and Margaret Preston. On my recommendation, Ossie began collecting Australian artists and convinced Jeremiah to allocate a portion of an upper shop floor for its display. Female artists would attract female customers and thus reinforce Frost's long-term trading strategy. Diners lunching at the revamped Frost canteen took the elevator to inspect the art and enjoy piano recitals staged to enhance the display. These small concerts became increasingly popular after a positive review in the Sunday papers. Davina Jenkins coordinated the guest list for a glittering premiere performance, attended by the Governor of New South Wales and documented in a lavish double page colour spread in a premium women's magazine.

Ossie said his wife told him it was time he realised black tie good taste trumped vulgar American trends. He took her criticism as a dig at being photographed with me, sitting on the front seat of his brand new Ambassador.

Though glowing magazine coverage provided a short-lived fillip, the overall financial prospects of the Frost chain remained bleak. Large, old Edwardian and Victorian buildings required constant maintenance. As part of a strategy of continuous improvement, Ossie recommended Jeremiah buy an IBM 7090, one of the original fully transistorised mainframes, capable of performing 229,000 calculations per second, and ideal for billing, payroll, and inventory control. But the impact of this advanced retail gadgetry unsettled loyal staff and made Jeremiah uneasy.

After scanning a single article in *Popular Mechanics*, Ossie realised an entire team of Frosties back office comptometers was no longer useful. Had Ashton lived to supervise these changes, I feel certain he would have developed a fair redeployment solution, but convincing Jeremiah to let go of long-term staff proved awkward.

Davina proposed that Oswald invite Jeremiah and Cornelia to a game of golf. In Davina's opinion, eight holes would be the perfect setting for a serious discussion about the emporium's future and the growing cost of maintaining Breffni, their expensive summer house at Mount Wilson in the Blue Mountains.

Though he had worked for the Frost Emporium for decades, Ossie mentioned to me he knew little about Jeremiah's life and heritage, other than his staunch commitment to Presbyterian values.

Both couples eventually agreed on a day on the greens of the Blackheath Golf Club, and, with Jeremiah's gruff reply of 'See you there next Saturday morning', Ossie drove to a garage on the Pacific Highway near Kissing Point Road to check the oil and inflate the Ambassador's tyres to the recommended pound per square inch unit of pressure.

A light dusting of sleet on the approach to Medlow Bath shortened the day. According to Ossie, Cornelia had invited them to stay the night at Breffni. Davina had agreed.

The snowfall decreased at the Mount Victoria turn-off and stopped as they approached the Darling Causeway. A mist rolling in from Mount Banks quelled Ossie's urge to evaluate the Ambassador's performance on the narrow curves and long straights.

The tattered state of the estate's grounds dismayed Ossie. English ivy and dark green holly bush made the gardens decrepit. His description intensified my sense of the passing of time. I remembered Breffni as the embodiment of style and grace in a setting suitable for a villa on the shores of Lake Como in Italy.

Cornelia struck a fire in the hearth while the men loaded lengths of dry split hardwood into a wheelbarrow, more than enough to keep the smallish sitting room toasty throughout the night. Ossie said the remainder of the house smelt damp and mouldy.

The women talked in the kitchen. Cornelia boiled chat potatoes. Davina prepared a white sauce for a side of cured ham and asparagus. Cornelia found a Christmas pudding, and Davina set about preparing a custard. Ossie said the aroma of cooking brought a slight feeling of elation to the dreary, vacant house, but otherwise he followed Jeremiah's lead and kept quiet. Apart from shouting commands in the woodshed, Jeremiah barely spoke more than a dozen sentences throughout the day, but hunger, a hearty meal and a glass of wine improved the old man's mood.

Ossie and I thought Jeremiah a teetotaller, but that night the old man said over the years he had learnt to enjoy the pleasures of the grape.

Ossie attempted to mimic Jeremiah's voice, saying, 'A wee brandy with warm water before bed grants me a few precious hours of sleep. At my age, four hours is a blessing. I find it hard to switch off. My doctor says wine in moderation and a tablespoon of diluted spirit is good for my heart.'

I laughed at Ossie's attempt at a Scots accent. In my mind's eye I imagined Jeremiah holding forth.

Cornelia pulled on a pair of leather gloves, prodded a log on the fire, and arranged peeled chestnuts to roast on glowing embers.

Ossie remarked that Cornelia thought her husband had changed over the years, particularly since Ashton's passing. She described the death of a child as beyond the normal scheme of things. Ossie later told me that Davina took his hand at this statement, the first sign of closeness between them in a long time.

Ossie's voice quavered as he described the impact of Ashton's death on Cornelia and Jeremiah. He described the sound of Cornelia prodding the coals and turning the blistering chestnuts with a pair of tongs as a metaphor for the couple's grief.

Jeremiah told Ossie he was not the man he once was, except for the constancy of his wife.

Ossie cleared his throat and sipped wine. To switch topics, he asked how the house came to be called 'Breffni'. He said he had never heard the word except when heading to the estate for the Christmas gatherings of years past.

Cornelia solved the mystery. The name Breffni came from her side of the family. According to Jeremiah, Cornelia was descended from royalty, a statement which reddened Davina's cheeks. She had assumed Cornelia was a distant relative of the Royal Family. But Cornelia informed Davina she was not related to the current residents of Buckingham Palace. Breffni was also an ancient empire in Ireland during the Middle Ages, and Cornelia a direct descendant of Hugh O'Neill, the Earl of Tyrone, and a destitute recipient of the Flight of the Earls. Yet somehow a dour old Scot like Jeremiah managed to win the heart of the most beautiful girl in Ulster. Cornelia claimed mutual respect was the secret ingredient of their marriage.

Ossie stood and turned to the fire to warm his hands. Cornelia and Davina went back to the kitchen to make the custard for the outdated Christmas pudding.

Jeremiah looked Ossie in the eye and, breaking the silence, proclaimed his wife a Catholic. Now it was Ossie's turn to feel heat in his cheeks, but before he could answer, Jeremiah explained Cornelia took the sacrament at St Mary's Cathedral whenever Cardinal Gilroy celebrated high mass.

While I was acutely aware of the deep religious divides across Australian society, I had never heard the nickname "Smiley Gilroy", who, according to Ossie's recollection of the discussion, was the finest man the old Presbyterian had ever met.

Ossie listened as Jeremiah recounted how he met Cardinal Gilroy sometime after Ashton's death.

The Cardinal gave a copy of John Henry Newman's "The Dream of Gerontius" to the inconsolable Jeremiah. Sometime afterwards, Ossie told me, the Cardinal invited Jeremiah to a performance of the poem set to the music of Sir Edward Elgar and performed in the crypt of St Mary's Cathedral.

Ossie said "The Dream of Gerontius" is the prayer of an old man on his deathbed, listening to angels and demons before passing.

Cornelia carried a tray with four bowls of steaming pudding. Davina, walking behind, held a large jug of custard. Cornelia asked what the two gentlemen were discussing. The peacefulness snow bestows settled as a blanket around the house. Clouds darkened a full winter moon. Flurries drifted in gusts, sweetening the quiet atmosphere. Hardwood smoke coiled as a genie within the hearth, warming the guests before joining the snowy corps de ballet for a pirouette in the silvered frost. Cornelia piled logs onto the roaring fire. Jeremiah stuffed Mac Baren's Scottish Blend into his briar pipe, picked up a small coal and set the tobacco alight.

'And what is it you need to talk to me about, Ossie?' he queried.

The accountant replied, 'Nothing of significance.'

Davina frowned at the shortening of her husband's name.

Realising time was slipping away, Cornelia said, 'Sing us a song, Jerry.'

Putting his pipe down, Jeremiah took hold of his wife's hand, got up, moved to the fire, and in a mellifluous tenor voice sang an old Jacobite tune.

> Sweet the laverock's note and lang.
> Liltin' wildly up the glen,
> but aye tae me he sings ae sang.
> 'Will ye no' come back again?'[20]

---

[20] After the defeat of Bonnie Prince Charlie at the Battle of Culloden, and his subsequent escape to France, thousands of Jacobites, who drew their support from the Catholic clans of the Scottish Highlands, yearned for his return. This version of the traditional air "Will Ye No' Come Back Again?" was written by Carolina Oliphant, known as Lady Nairne, in the first half of the 19th century.

20 Broken butterfly

At a routine check-up, my doctor asked if I suffered with night terrors. My blood pressure was too high and sleep paralysis, he said, signalled depression and anxiety.

Indeed, during those frightful nights, and before I started yoga, I would sit up in bed, screaming and babbling nonsense. My heart thumped in my chest.

There were times I felt the need to protect myself and escape a fearful threat. Minutes or hours passed until I came to, dripping sweat, sometimes standing in a corner. I cannot recall details of the nightmares and, since practicing yoga daily, I thought I had rid myself of nocturnal panic. Not so.

My telephone's chime melded into a threatening narrative. Somehow, though trapped in a cowl of sleep, I knew the rhythm of the ring was something worse.

Stanley Hull remained a steadfast if seldom seen friend, but it took several minutes for him to answer my repeated question.

'Tell me who is speaking, or I'll hang up.'

'It is my sister Deborah. She's dead.'

I could not tell whether this was a nightmare or reality. Time stretched from silence to words and back again.

'Where are you?'

'St Vincent's Emergency Department, Darlinghurst.'

I felt outside my being, watching as I dressed and examining a wooden comb I had never seen before. I grabbed my car keys, and, in the light of the full moon, drove along Darlinghurst Road at 4 am, and found a miracle parking spot near the Cutler Footway. Somehow, I came to be by Stanley's side among coughing, wheezing, wounded people, balancing private pain in a public space.

Stanley sat catatonic, chest across his knees, in a posture of desperate grief. 'I have to identify her body.'

Questions screamed in my head. Where is she? How could this be Deborah? This is not real.

I am not strong. I avoid the limelight. I do not lead. I seek shadows where I work silently on this project, or that design, yet beside me sits a friend with no hope for tomorrow. But tomorrow is here, and the dawn shoos away splinters of moonlight, glinting in sprayed puddles.

As the night shift ends, so the day shift began.

A lilting Irish voice asked, 'How do youse have your tea?', and I bit into a soft egg and lettuce sandwich and swallowed strong, black, sweet tea.

A grey-haired registrar roused Stanley from his grief.

'Are you ready, Mr Hull?'

'Yes, I think so.'

'It will only take a moment.'

'Can my friend come?'

The registrar asked if I was family.

'I am not,' I said. 'But I will be here when you return, Stan. I promise.' I watched as they disappeared behind heavy winged doors. The hissing draught reeked of ether and vomit. I felt sick and walked to the exit. Sweet, wet air wafted from Green Park. Workers strolled two by two toward the spired city. Art students smoked cigarettes as they called to one another. Traffic became heavier. Ambulances with flashing lights came and went.

When I returned, the registrar, sitting at Stanley's side, spoke in a soft, matter-of-fact voice.

'It was difficult, Miss ...'

'Susan Lieder.'

'I suggest you try to get some rest. The police will contact Mr Hull and advise him if a coronial inquest is necessary. It is hospital policy to wait for the coroner's finding before issuing a death certificate.'

'The police?'

'I am afraid so. Abortion is illegal in New South Wales. My initial finding shows Miss Hull's death is the result of a crime. If circumstances were different, we would not be having this conversation. I hope the day comes when the government heeds the advocacy of Dr Wainer in Victoria, and these backyard butchers are arrested.'

Stanley asked, 'Are you saying the newspapers will run this as a story?'

'That depends on the journalist covering the Coroner's Court on the day, Mr Hull. We are facing a backlog of deaths by abortion, so it could be months before the matter is heard. In the meantime, I suggest you inform your family and begin funeral arrangements. The hospital will be in touch.

'We retrieved these items from your sister's body,' the registrar added, handing Stanley a brown paper bag. 'I am sorry for your loss.'

Stanley rummaged through the contents, retrieved an object, and handed it to me. Sweat on my palm moistened the bejewelled Monarch butterfly pendant, brightening the diamonds dotted on the body, the head and the wings. I noticed one of the two swallowtails missing, snapped from the bottom of the brooch.

'What happened here?'

'A bloody diamond for a souvenir,' Stanley said. 'The bastard didn't know its value. Why fucking break it?'

And the day became the afternoon shift, and a lady with a Spanish accent offered coffee and biscuits and pointed out the public bathrooms.

I had lost all sense of time but could not abide the thought of abandoning Deborah in a cold hospital ward.

Stanley talked nonstop, describing her later years; a sequence of experiences far removed from the girl I knew. We had remained in touch by phone, but when we spoke, she was either drunk or incoherent or crying about a drama in her private life. I lost patience ages ago, and the guilt of my heartlessness took my breath away.

Stanley recalled details of a life remote from her teen years and twenties – behaviour at odds with the bright, vivacious person I first met in Breffni in Mount Wilson.

'She moved out of the pied-à-terre our parents bought in Potts Point and found digs in a boarding house over the bridge in Waverton. We lost contact for a year till she rang me from Glebe, of all places. She was in a terrible state. A moll in a pub on Glebe Point Road accused her of flirting with her husband and beat her senseless. The ambulance took her to Royal Prince Alfred Hospital with a broken arm and a busted nose.

'I tried calling, but you were on the high seas somewhere. After discharge, she moved into a flat in Petersham. She was hostile and warned me to stay the fuck out of her life. She piled on weight. Spent much of her time in pubs around Stanmore and Marrickville, going from one drinking session to another. She was never short of money. Our parents gave her an allowance and left her alone.' He gave a dejected hunch of his shoulders. 'And now this. I don't know who the bloke was, but there was no way she was going to have a baby if the father wasn't Ashton, and it killed her.' Stanley's shoulders heaved with sobs.

I had to escape the stale tobacco smell. Sirens wailed outside. A barely visible white moon rose over the brightening Paddington rooftops. Sleep might let the anxiety dissipate.

When I returned, Stanley was arguing with an attendant. 'I don't believe you,' he yelled.

'What's going on?' I demand of the flustered nurse. 'We're about to leave, so please tell me what is happening.'

'You can forget going anywhere near Taylor Square,' she said. 'Oxford Street is blocked. The old Frost Emporium building near Hyde Park is on fire.'

My heart thumped. I gulped air. I had to get away or fight, but I could do neither.

21 Chief of Staff

I am proud of my ability to focus on the task at hand. When not working, I pass my days and nights enjoying fine music. No matter how many times I listen, I lose myself in the maze of intertwining instruments and am convinced J. S. Bach's *Art of Fugue* is a dialogue of angels, whether played on solo piano or by a quartet.

I see art in four dimensions, the last of which – the passage of time – coaxed from my immersion in an accomplished canvas or objet d'art. Art is central to my existence, but since my stay in Hay I have become distracted. I drive from the humdrum of Commonwealth Street to the jacarandas of Seaforth, and the gentian blue of Middle Harbour, and repeat ad infinitum.

I am fortunate to have my portfolio of watercolours curated in a handful of Paddington galleries. Sales cover the price of paint, canvas and framing, plus the forty per cent commission. I enjoy opening nights, the gossip, the catered dinners with gallerists and friends. I listen and learn from the conversations about art, which often end in furious debate about Australia being a so-called cultural desert.

Each month, another acquaintance sails or flies to England, or Europe or the United States or Canada, never to return. But I cannot join them. I dread a knock on my door by a federal official, demanding clarification of my identity.

Some years ago, I had a nasty run in with an immigration officer in Darwin when I returned from a sailing trip to Bali. Luckily, he waved me through on a stern warning that I renew my travel documents, but I have done nothing about this since my last intimidating meeting with an intelligence bureaucrat in Canberra.

There is not a day when I do not think about Leo's letters. I am obsessed with the arcane calligraphy on the envelopes, and the letter with the Bulgarian postmark, with nothing inside. My pet name, ZaSu, and a return address on the back flap, makes me think it is from Leo, but the script is nothing like the handwriting in his note from the internment camp. Despite the big public to-do in Hay, which I am convinced would have reached the eyes and ears of my interrogators, I have heard nothing more, and bleak depression tightens like a scarf wound around my throat.

I am falling behind in design contracts, cutting back on new commissions. My income is plummeting. I fret about cash flow and the rising cost of living. I am contemplating retirement and devoting my time to art and my patronage of the New Theatre and the Conservatorium of Music. But I yearn to return to England and Europe to face the truth of what I instinctively know.

A letter from the Australian Parliament summoning me to Canberra for a briefing is emblematic of this conundrum. Weeks after the train trip to the national capital, a transcript of the interview arrived in my letter box.

'Thank you for coming, Miss Liebler. I am Aldo Gabriel, Chief of Staff for the Minister of State Security. Beatrice Charles is taking notes of the meeting, which will run as long as required. I hope you do not have any plans because—'

'Pardon the interruption, Mr Gabriel, but my surname is Lieder, not Liebler.'

'That is not true. Your real name is Shoshanna Liebler, and you are known as Susan Lieder. This is correct, isn't it? And it is the reason for this conversation.'

'Am I in trouble, Mr Gabriel?'

'You might be, Miss Liebler. We will discuss this later, but for now, I need to confirm your identity.'

'May I ask how these matters came about? I have done nothing wrong, nor broken any laws. I pay my taxes and live quietly, and yet here I am in a minister's office, discussing issues relevant only to me. I deserve an explanation about why I am here.'

'Your presence today is the result of a formal representation on your behalf by a person or persons whom the Minister holds in high regard. Before I go into details, I need to be absolutely sure you are Shoshanna Liebler.'

'Yes, I am.'

'And born in Vienna on this date?'

'Yes.'

'Yet your British Overseas Passport lists a different surname, date and place of birth verified on the manifest of the vessel on which you arrived in Australia. Is this correct?'

'Yes.'

'So, you lied when you entered this country?'

'Yes.'

'Why did you do this? And why do you go by the name Lieder?'

'Because it is the married name of my father's sister, my aunt.'

'But why did you travel on this name, and not your real name?'

'Lieder means "songs" in German, and my aunt's husband, my uncle, is not Jewish. At the time of my departure for Australia, it was wise to have a surname which would not attract attention.'

'So was your employer at the Frost Emporium aware of your deception?'

'No, but I refute your broad insinuation.'

'Why?'

'Because both my aunt and uncle are an integral part of my family's business.'

'And were you eighteen when you landed in Darling Harbour and not twenty-one?'

'Yes.'

'It is important you know this because the Australian Parliament recently amended the *Commonwealth Electoral Act of 1918*, lowering the minimum voting age to eighteen years.'

'How does this apply to me? I have never voted in Australia.'

'You realise voting is compulsory? I'll need to check the statutes, but when you entered Australia at age eighteen, you were a minor, and subject to different interpretations of law. I will come back to this later, but Miss Charles points out this might go in your favour.'

'Favour for what?'

'I am reluctant to name names, but the person or persons making representations on your behalf believes you are entitled to the benefit of the doubt apropos your illegal entry to this country. My role is to elicit relevant information so the Minister can decide.'

'Decide what?'

'Whether to prosecute and deport you or grant full citizenship. The information you provide today is critical to your future. Do you understand the magnitude of what I am saying?'

'Yes.'

'Then allow me to return to my original question. Why did you lie to an Australian Immigration official, and why did you travel to this country on forged documents?'

'I am Jewish, Mr Gabriel, and have a long memory. I recall my father reading news reports about thousands of English Jews joining Irish dock workers, communists, members of the British Labour Party, trade unionists and the people of London's East End, to fight the police and stop Oswald Mosley's British Union of Fascists marching along Cable Street. This was 1936, the same year Emperor Haile Selassie of Ethiopia, living in exile in the City of Bath, tried to alert the British government of the horrors of Mussolini's atrocities in his country. His warnings were ignored. Two years later in the weeks after I sailed to Australia, the Third Reich swallowed my country whole, and began the extermination of almost the entire Jewish population of Austria and Europe. But before the war, tens of thousands of Jews trying to flee Europe were denied entry to many countries. I'm sure you are familiar with the fate of those aboard the SS *St Louis*. My parents knew the risks, and when I had an opportunity to come to Australia, my family did whatever was necessary to ensure my safe passage in the hope of joining me here one day. But this has not eventuated.

'Great Britain was in chaos after the abdication scandal. And I am sure you know that in 1937 the Duke of Windsor toured Germany with his American wife, who took tea with Rudolph Hess. The Duke's behaviour was treasonous, so do not lecture me about the illegality of my entry, sir, when a man who almost became our head of state, and whose family Australians still revere, betrayed his country and the British Empire, to the Nazis.'

'Let's take a break.'

Morning tea concluded. Interview resumes, 11.15am. Aldo Gabriel, Beatrice Charles, and Shoshanna Liebler, present.

'Are you aware of matters recorded in your ASIO file?'

'What is an ASIO file?'

'I can tell you your file is as extensive as it is mundane.'

'What does it say about me?'

'The details are highly personal. Someone close to you reported on every aspect of your life, none of which has the slightest bearing on the rationale for keeping the file.'

'My god.'

'The outcome of this assessment is binary. This means the Australian government will keep your ASIO file active, if legal action proceeds, but if there is no prosecution, you can access it and peruse its contents. Let's continue. Did you contribute to Australia's war effort?'

'Yes.'

'How?'

'I am not at liberty to say.'

'Why?'

'Because I signed the *Official Secrets Act*. I have never breached my pledge to remain silent about my war work and will not do so now. I believe in the inviolability of an oath, and besides, I know you have access to the details of my work during the war.'

'May I ask about your relationship with a Mr Leo Hulbert?'

'Leo is a trusted family assistant and was my bodyguard during our voyage to Australia. We lost touch after our arrival in Australia when he was arrested and sent to an internment camp in Hay.'

'So, Mr Hulbert was aware of your true age?'

'Yes.'

'I am going to show you a document. This is a New South Wales Police travel permit issued to Mr Hulbert. Do you recognise the name?'

'Yes. May I ask if you have any other information about Mr Hulbert?'

'We have a receipt from the British government marked "SOE", for a travel permit to the United Kingdom, and Australian documents noting his internment as an enemy alien, plus a police assault and battery charge on an immigration official. The travel permit is the last official document naming Mr Hulbert, I am afraid.'

'I see. Is there anything else I can help you with, sir?'

'No, you are free to go.'

'Will I hear from you again?'

'You can expect one of two outcomes following this discussion: a summons to appear in the Federal Court to answer charges laid by the Australian Department of Immigration, or an invitation to a citizenship ceremony where you will be granted full rights as an Australian in the name Shoshanna Liebler. If the latter outcome occurs, you may apply to change your name to Susan Lieder by deed poll.'

'Do I get to meet the Minister?'

'No, but be assured, this government will keep Australia safe from threats from all quarters of the political spectrum, and from people at home and abroad. Miss Charles will see you out. Thank you for your cooperation.'

***

I check my letterbox two or three times a day, but apart from this transcript of the interview, which I re-read in the vain hope of uncovering a clue about my fate, I still know nothing of Leo's whereabouts, and decades have passed since I have heard from my family. I ask myself: did I betray my family and my heritage so I could live comfortably in Australia? Perhaps so.

The dreadful night terrors return, and worse still, there is no-one in whom I can confide. I have never felt so alone in my life.

22 The interpretation of nightmares

And if our sense of time has grown weary with age or was
never all that strongly developed – a sign of an inborn lack
of vitality – it very soon falls asleep again, and within twenty
four hours it is as if we were never gone, and our journey
were merely last night's dream.

– Thomas Mann

I am an avid collector of bric-a-brac and ephemera, but hand
on heart I declare my most treasured possessions are my
citizenship certificate and passport. Thanks to an unknown
advocate, I am free to travel wherever I choose. Despite, or
because of, recent travails, I decided to return to Austria to learn
my family's fate.

I didn't tell any of my friends about my journey, nor did
I mention my motivation, for I am a true-born Austrian, and
hiding one's emotions is a national pastime. Little wonder
Sigmund Freud wrote *The Interpretation of Dreams* in this city, a
book which gave the world the concepts of id, ego and superego.

Vienna's most beautiful boulevard, the Ringstraße, remains
a lodestone for artists, composers and authors. And let us not
forget the city's pious and pompous who glorify God in palaces
and churches so ornate a French word entered the lexicon to
describe their opulence: rococo.

I had forgotten the symbolism of the imperial double-
headed eagle gazing in two directions. And if I am to look back
on Vienna, a camouflaged, scarred city, I decided an interlocutor
might help guide me through the streets of my youth.

I chose obscurity in my adult life. Now, upon returning
to the dreamworld of my past, I realise the unknowable will
be revealed, and thus girded, I can face my mortality with
equanimity.

I dialled a number listed in a tourist brochure. A man answered in different languages, each phrase translating to 'Anton speaking. How may I help you?'

'Where do you meet your clients?'

'Do you prefer German or English madam ... *Liebe Dame?*' he asked.

'Either,' I replied. 'I am fluent in seven languages.'

'Do I detect an accent, madam? Are you English?'

'Australian.'

'There is a bistro called the Roo Bar. Shall we meet there?'

I sensed a smile in his voice. 'The Shakespeare & Company bookshop is more to my taste.'

'Yes, I know it. Close to Marc-Aurel-Straße. We can have coffee and tailor a tour to your needs. And your name, madam?'

'Shoshanna Liebler, but you may call me ZaSu.'

I strained to hear an intake of breath, but he spoke with aplomb, for I am just another tourist keen to use his service to take in the sights.

'And how will I know you, Herr Anton?'

'By my beard and moustache.' He chuckled and asked, 'What is a suitable time to meet?'

'Three o'clock?'

'See you then,' he said, and clicked off the phone.

I browsed the shelves for books by authors I recognised. *Chess: The Royal Game,* a novel by Stefan Zweig, stood out. I reached for an edition with cover art in the Constructionist style, thumbed its pages and read these words:

> They were no longer two opponents wanting to test
> each other's playing skills, but two enemies who had
> sworn to annihilate each other.

Stefan's father, Moritz Zweig, a reputable Viennese textile manufacturer, was a friend of my father. A pang churned my stomach. I chose another book I had seen in a second-hand book shop in Hobart: *The Last Voyage of Aratus,* the story of a man desperate to atone for his Great Sin.

I looked up from the cover artwork by the Japanese print master Tsukioka Yoshitoshi. 'You have read this?'

'Australian books are rare in Austria,' he said.

'Herr Anton, I presume.'

'At your service, madam,' he replied, taking my hand with a slight bow and a brief movement of bewhiskered lips toward my fingers. I could not recall when I last experienced this courtesy. Australians shake hands, or wave toward the person to whom they have been introduced.

I stepped back to size up my guide. A clipped goatee with flecked brown and grey hairs formed a neat hirsute triangle under his chin. A similar coloured moustache, curled and waxed into twirls, coiled toward ruddy cheekbones, framing eyes of the brightest ultramarine. Creases and wrinkles suggested a life far beyond my three score and ten. He stood erect, dressed in a worn Harris Tweed jacket, offset with a dun-coloured oilskin cape and olive green moleskin trousers. A tie pin affixed a cravat around his throat. His clothes suggested a *flâneur*[21] down on his luck, for his shoes, though polished, were worn at the heels.

'I drive a *janschky*[22] from Albertinaplatz to the Heldenplatz[23] of the Hofburg Palace,' he said. 'In summer, it proves a handy supplement. You would be surprised by the number of people who ask to look at the balcony of the Neue Burg wing.'

'But it is closed to the public, yes?' I remark, before asking, 'And do you point it out?'

'Depends on the size of their gratuity. I am a lifelong habitué of Heidinger's *Gasthaus,*[24] and a generous tip means I eat my fill with *mein gastgeber,*'[25] he said, leaning on a slender walnut walking stick.

---

[21] stroller
[22] horse-drawn carriage
[23] Our Hero's Square
[24] inn
[25] my host

'Does it not bother you, Herr Anton?' I enquired.

He shrugged.

'One or two tourists ask to visit the Vienna Museum to view the panorama of the city etched after the Turkish siege of 1529. Others ask for the location on the Danube where German pikemen hacked Ottomans to pieces with their two-handed swords and tossed the remains into the river.'

'And do you oblige?'

'The Danube is not blue, madam, but if they offer a good tip, I take them to the Floridsdorf Bridge and turn it red with stories of the blood of decapitated janissaries. The more knowledgeable ask about the bridge's contemporary history and are thrilled with my description of a recent slaughter. A guide must keep his clients happy.'

'And which tour do you recommend for me?'

He picked up a book at random, fanned the pages, placed it on a pile, and smiled. 'A midnight tour departs Albertinaplatz on the first chime of the Pummerin Bell. Tomorrow is the Feast of Pentecost, a perfect time to visit the Seven Sights. You may choose from one of four carriages. I supply a fresh ermine throw and schnapps to ward off the cold. Tell me, ZaSu, is Vienna your last stop, or do you travel elsewhere in Europe?'

'I am curious about Bulgaria,' I said.

'A peek at life beyond the Iron Curtain before you return to Australia, eh?'

'You never know who you'll meet behind a door unless you knock. And are other guests joining us this evening, Herr Anton?'

'Just you, ZaSu.'

I chose warm clothes, and a headscarf kept in place by mother's hatpin, which I had retrieved from Leo's strongbox in Hay. A hatpin, Mama once reminded me, though small, can be, if required, a bejewelled dagger.

Despite the lateness, I walked from my hotel through the Inner Ring to the Heldenplatz. A brisk pace helps my circulation, but, as I passed the Hoher Market with its Anchor Clock, the road lights dimmed, causing my shadow to stretch and circle as I moved from one pool of light to the next. The disorienting flicker from darkness to dazzle tingled the hairs on the nape of my neck. Was it the chill air on my cheek?

As I approached Michaelerplatz and the Spanish Riding School, with the carriage assembly point nearby, a distended shadow appeared from the dark. An old man approached, clutching a cluster of toy balloons in one hand, and maintaining his balance with a walking stick in the other.

'Liebe Dame, ein ballon?'[26] he asked, placing the crook of the stick on his wrist, and stretching his other hand toward me. I fumbled for a coin, placed it in his palm, and took the string. The man saluted, and accompanied by his unsteady shadow, tottered into the darkness.

The Pummerin Bell chimed time.

Anton motioned me to grasp his arm, but I demurred.

'Welcome to my humble tour,' he said, fastening the balloon to a strut by the driver's bench. 'As I am to be your guide,' he continued, 'Herr Alois has kindly agreed to take the reins of our horse for this evening.'

I noticed the driver's ragged boots spiralled at the toes, and a battered top hat secured a scarf wound around his neck and head.

'The poor man lives with the Sisters of Charity, don't you, Alois?' Anton said. 'A Molotov cocktail burnt off his face. Time to go.'

The bass peal of St Stephen's Pummerin reverberated.

Anton sat facing me in the carriage, his back to Alois.

'The new bell weighs over twenty tonnes, and like the old Pummerin, the heads of Ottoman are carved into the support brackets at the top of the belfry. Am I not a knowledgeable guide, ZaSu? The bell is rung on special occasions such as tonight,' he said, but I interjected before he continued.

---

[26] Dear lady, a balloon?

'And do you know Pentecost is a Jewish harvest festival, observed on the fiftieth day from the second day of Passover? So, it seems, the Holy Spirit not only entered the Apostles, but nurtured them as well.'

'Now the guest is guiding the guide,' Anton replied.

I leant against the plush backrest and tucked the ermine throw below my knees. The carriage swayed. Hooves echoed on darkened cobblestones.

'Drive on,' Anton said. 'The Seven Sights Tour of Vienna tells the story of the siege of our city from within and above. Until the very end, war came from the sky. Americans by day, British by night. To protect Vienna, the Germans built six flak towers. Ugly, horrible structures, which some believe secure six of the Seven Seals of the *Book of Revelation*. The towers acted as air raid shelters for thousands of Viennese during the bombing raids.

'The brigades drove into the towers' basements, to douse the incendiary fires, and hose out the shit, vomit and blood in time for the next raid. The dead were tossed into the embers.'

And I saw towers in the Augarten in the second district, one in the Arenberg Park in the third district, another in Esterhazypark in the sixth district, and the Stiftskaserne in the seventh district.

'Tracer shells filled the night sky, far brighter than any shower of meteors. Million candle-watt searchlights fingered heaven, and enemy aircraft fell as flaming angels into the Vienna Woods, only to return the following night to bomb Vienna once more, or Budapest, or Bucharest.

'Thousands upon thousands of lumbering avengers spewed white condensation trails as they passed above.

'Then, in the spring of 1945, the Bolsheviks fell upon us in two waves. Tens of millions of their steel locusts devoured much of the city, chewing the mortar from between the bricks before moving on, as the buildings collapsed into dust and rubble.

'The end came on April 10 when Das Reich abandoned the bridge in the 21st district. Bloated bodies polluted the Danube at Floridsdorf. The following day, Vienna became a Soviet town.

'Within a week, the Bolsheviks advanced to other parts of Austria, as the Third Ukrainian Front swept on to Berlin. Drive on, Alois.'

The carriage passed the Schwarzenbergplatz with its semicircular white marble colonnade.

'This is the Heroes Monument to the Red Army. More than 17,000 Soviet soldiers died in the Battle for Vienna, and those who survived and occupied the city were aged thirteen or less. Armed, emaciated kids from Central Asia, dressed in uniforms too big for skinny bodies, helmets like upturned cooking pots on their heads, and boots stuffed with rags to bind their feet and legs.

'Night and day, drunken gangs goaded their comrades to rape any girl who crossed their path. Virgin youths, so enraged with sexual inadequacy, bashed innumerable women to death. The carnage continued until Soviet political commissars took control of the administration of the city. I lost count of the number of civilians and rapists shot each night. Posters plastered onto the remains of buildings read:

> Comrades: do not behave like Nazis. Be merciless
> towards German enslavers, but do not offend the
> Austrian population. Respect their traditions, families,
> and private property. Proudly carry the glorious title of
> a Red Army warrior. Let your conduct cause respect
> everywhere for the Red Army.

'But few, if any, of the perpetrators could read. Red Army soldiers raped between 70,000 and 100,000 women in Vienna.

'After Dr Renner formed a provisional government, a sort of order calmed the city and we citizens managed to scrounge for food in a modicum of peace, but famine marched in lockstep behind the conqueror.

'Drive on, Alois,' Anton said again. 'Penzinger Straße.'

I felt sick but, determined to keep my dignity, and like a true-born Viennese, deny these men the satisfaction of seeing an old lady weep.

Over the decades, I pieced together my parents' fate, but I had to see with my own eyes the brass plaque embedded in the footpath in front of my old house and touch its cold truth. German text revealed the names of my Papa and Mama – Maximillian and Ruth Liebler – their date of birth and probable date of murder in the Mauthausen concentration camp, west of Vienna. I do not know for certain, but I suspect the Gestapo arrested my parents on that fateful trip to Trieste because the road they travelled passes through the city of Linz. Tens of thousands of these heartbreaking memorials testify to the aftermath of *Kristallnacht,*[27] each a talisman of love, loss, and memory.

Anton proffered a tumbler of schnapps as I re-entered the carriage. I called for another.

'Drive on, Alois.'

Though the tour was ending, I knew nothing of Rudolph's fate, and asked Anton about the destiny of displaced persons.

'Millions remain missing,' he replied, 'and as the decades pass, many exist only as memories.'

'I remember my brother Rudolph set off for Odessa before the Anschluss,' I said.

Anton offered another tumbler of schnapps, and, when I refused, he drank the liquor in a gulp. 'I recall a newspaper report of Soviet officials requesting the help of Austrian forensic scientists to identify human bones found in the catacombs beneath Odessa.

'This was during the thaw of the Khrushchev years, after Stalin's death. The Soviets maintained a cordial relation of sorts

[27] The Night of Crystal or The Night of Broken Glass

with the Austrian Republic to keep their spies safe from prying Americans.

'Austrian authorities insisted all documentation accompany the remains, to help expedite the identification. I do not recall a name but recollect the report of a peculiar feature found on the forehead of the skull.

'The scientists noticed an emblem inscribed on the bone above the nose. As near as they could discern, it outlined a dagger through the Hammer and Sickle, the symbol of the NKVD.'

Anton poured another tumbler of schnapps, which I all but snatched from his grasp.

During our outbound journey to Australia, Leo talked about a run-in he and Rudolph had with a gang of NKVD apparatchiks in Odessa's outskirts.

'Why do the English say, "jump to conclusions"?' I said aloud.

Anton's words resonated in my imagination, and without further investigation or evidence, I decided his story summarised my brother's fate.

'Drive on, Alois. To Heldenplatz'.

A pale first light of Pentecost glowed in the east, banishing the threatening shadows. Other than cawing blackbirds fluttering the length of the empty square, the clip-clopping hooves echoed our arrival in the empty plaza.

'People climbed the statue of Prince Eugene of Savoy to get a closer view, and who could blame them?' Anton exclaimed. 'A half-million Austrians crammed into this square, chanting *Seig Heil, Seig Heil.* Our day of liberation had come. This is what we were told. I believed. All Austrians believed.'

Too much schnapps emboldened Anton to stray from his normal tourist patter. Clearly, he did not feel threatened by an old Jewish woman. I decided not to silence him with the taunt of withholding the coveted gratuity.

'You are familiar with the British, are you not, Madam ZaSu?' he asked. Anton's eyes glowed the closer we came to the Neue Burg wing.

'Go on, Anton,' I nodded.

'"They are a remarkably stupid, thick-headed people. The British follow the principle that when you lie, lie big, and stick to it. They keep up their lies, even at the risk of looking ridiculous." Do you know who said these words?'

'And you are telling me this wasn't a lie?' I replied, pointing toward the Neue Burg balcony.

Early morning joggers zigged and zagged the wide grey Heldenplatz.

'And I suppose you believe in the bigger American lie of "manifest destiny", with its endless expansion. Westward Ho,' Anton said, cupping his hand to his mouth and miming the cracking of a whip. 'A bunch of rich Masons and Rosicrucians dreamt up that nonsense. Now their descendants flock to Vienna in their thousands to gaze at the precise location where our liberation was proclaimed.'

Anton quoted a passage of St John the Divine:

> And when he had opened the seventh seal, there was
> silence in heaven about the space of half an hour. And
> I saw the seven angels who stood before him, and to
> them were given seven trumpets. Then the seven angels
> who had the seven trumpets prepared to sound them.
> The first angel sounded his trumpet, and there came
> hail and fire mixed with blood, and it was hurled down
> upon the earth.

'Mozart was a Mason,' I said.

'Shut up, you Jewish whore and say the Führer's name,' Anton demanded.

I leant across the carriage, placed the tip of my mother's hatpin at the side of Anton's head, and thrust into his flesh. A fine trickle of blood disappeared into his beard.

'There is a word in Middle English which describes the precise location on your skull where you now feel this sharp point. The word is *templ*, from the Latin *templum*, an open or consecrated space. You realise the temple is the shortest, easiest path to your brain, Anton? You have allowed this desecration to fester for too long.' I tapped on his skull. 'And now the time has come to bring this to an end.'

'You have killed before, ZaSu?' Anton asked.

'No, but you have.'

Anton slumped in the sumptuous carriage seat, his ravaged face pale as the insipid sun. Shards of wax fell like dandruff from his moustache, soiling his cravat.

I stepped from the carriage and handed up the envelope containing the tip.

'Vergessen Sie ihren ballon nicht liebe Dame.'[28]

'Drive on, Alois,' I said.

---

[28] Do not forget your balloon, dear lady.

23 Rust

> Blessed are You, God, Ruler of the universe,
> who creates the fruit of the vine.

Look at the veins in my arms, Rudolph. A river of venous blood pulses around my wrists. My cardinal points tingle as my blood flows past the blockage in my heart. The iron grip behind my left breast has subsided and I can breathe at last, but drums pound in my ears.

Let us step outside for fresh air, dear brother, before the paperboy comes. He is always late. He is a sweet youth with a sunny smile for us older women. I love the sound of the trill of his whistle. Walk with me, brother. The hill is steep, and I cannot feel the soles of my feet, but I will glide by your side and rest my head on your shoulder. I will nap this afternoon while you play "Surabaya Johnny", the version sung by Lotte Lenya. Let us see what is happening in the world.

Do you recall when our Papa brought us to the Burgenland plains? Remember when he and Mama stocked our cellar with the best vintage of the season? The wine merchants wore smart woollen traditional hats, with emerald-green velvet lapels adorning their suits. Similar coloured stripes followed the outside seams of their trousers. Each man greeted Papa as an old friend, but in truth they called 'come hither' to every stroller. I remember how their moustaches coiled to ruddy cheeks and smile-creased eyes, how they poured generous sample glasses held to the sun to enhance the colour. Passers-by could not resist, and succumbed to their patter, and, after gurgling quaffs and a bite of rye bread with a morsel of acidulous cheese, moved on to the next vintner.

Papa's favourite tipple, pressed from the local grape variety, thrives in a handful of vineyards near the town of Mönchhof on the far side of Neusiedler Lake. He said conditions must be perfect if the grape is to yield an ideal tirage. If this occurred, the bin of an exemplary year is prized by connoisseurs, and our Papa is a true cognoscente.

A particular type of microbe flourishes in the Burgenland soil, Papa said, and multiplies when frost reaches a precise intensity. Spring rains must fall at a definite time, and summer heat be just so.

Fields of sunflowers grow along the banks of the Danube from the outskirts of Bratislava to the walls of the town of Parndorf. Full-faced flowers bend as one in the breeze, turning with the passing sun, the yellow so intense in the afterglow, it lingers in my eye-shut sight.

The vignerons and vintners charted the behaviour of wild storks. If the fledglings attempt flight too soon, or seasonal storms batter the rooks atop the sloping slate roofs of the village houses, a vintage might fail.

Do you recall exploring that reed thicket down by the shingle? You found a stork's nest and took hold my hand to show off your discovery. I cried at the sight of the dead fledgling. You held me in your arms and promised a sorbet from the pastry shop near the Fisherman's Church. Inside, you said, are pious murals painted by forgotten hands in the early years of the Holy Roman Empire. But I was too frightened to go inside, terrified by stories of a bloodied man hanging on a cross. We ate our ice creams on a sun-warmed bench in front of a winery.

A humid wind blew from the west. Dark clouds built to a bruised purple on the far horizon of Neusiedler Lake.

The fledglings spread downy wings to catch the breeze, jumping and landing, impatient for the roiling zephyr to carry them skyward. But, as the turbulence passed, they loosed disappointed squelches of snowy guano onto the sloping rooftops.

We walked hand in hand to the town hall square and found Papa and Mama eating goulash soup served in a crusty bread bowl.

The Haydn Cellar Quartet welcomed four special guests. With the opening chords of the *Wind Octet in F Major*, tipsy laughter muffled the adolescent birds' frustrated honking.

Mama said Austrians and Hungarians claimed Rust, an old Saxon village from the 12th century, in the year the Fisherman's Church was consecrated to those who harvest grapes grown on the shores of Neusiedler Lake. Papa said Voltaire derided all the old duchies hereabouts, as neither holy, Roman nor part of an empire.

Papa and Mama laughed, drank and chit-chatted with acquaintances in Magyar and German. The notes of the wind octet serenaded the deepening twilight.

Sleep crept late during those long summer days, and as darkness stalked midnight's stroke, I played and played on the shoreside carnival rides, until slumber cascaded around me, and I forgot the day's jumble.

The odour of sweat is pungent on your shirt, as you carry drowsy me to our apartment in the Seehotel. And, as I fall asleep, lulled by viola and violin, I dream I am flying with a band of young storks to their marshy feeding places in far-off African savannahs.

Printed in Great Britain
by Amazon

52180027R00088